I0817817

-THE LEGEND OF HULLABEE ISLAND-

GENEVA SOMMERS

and the First Fairytales

-THE LEGEND OF HULLABEE ISLAND-

GENEVA SOMMERS

and the First Fairytales

C.J. BENJAMIN

For information regarding permission, write to:
Attention: Crown Atlantic Publishing
2000 Mariposa Vista Lane #104
St. Augustine, FL 32084

Published in the United States by Crown Atlantic Publishing

ISBN 978-1-7326123-9-6

Version 1.1
Printed in the United States of America
First edition printed, January 2019

This collection of stories is
dedicated to the fans.

Thank you for all your love and support
of The Geneva Project and the beloved
characters that drive this series. You've helped me mold my
imaginary musings into
the heroes we can all see within ourselves.
The Prequel series is for you.

Keep dreaming, aspiring, climbing;
your imagination is limitless.

VOLCANO
RAINFOREST
N

ISLAND
Tower
-of-
Lux
Lux
Troian Center

The Christmas Gift

A SHORT STORY

C.J. Benjamin

1

Remi polished the dull silver metal until it gleamed. He was almost able to make out the pattern engraved into the metal disc when a Grift approached. Startled, Remi quickly pocketed the artifact. His face flushed instantly and his heart hammered in his chest. He'd never done something illegal before. All items recovered from the Flood were the property of the city of Lux. His only job as an orphan at the Troian Center was to collect, polish and turn over his findings each and every day; and he always complied. He knew if he didn't it would mean a sentence in the locker. Even knowing the rules, he couldn't explain it, there was something special about the hunk of metal he'd just found and he couldn't part with it.

The Grift snatched the items Remi already deposited into his collection basket and moved on. Remi looked over his shoulder to where his best friend was perched on the rubble pile – Jane #65. Her wild blonde hair stuck out of her ponytail in unruly curls. Her shirttail was untucked and her bony shoulder stuck out of the oversized neck hole, but she looked like she was in her glory as her nimble fingers sifted through the piles of debris. He couldn't believe it'd been almost a year since they were assigned to Flood work. It was by far the best job they'd had as orphans. It definitely beat laundry and kitchen duty. 65 loved Flood work. But then again, she always loved when they got to do something new. Remi wondered how long it would be before the novelty wore off.

In just a few weeks it would be time for the New Year Gala and all the orphans in his year would officially turn nine-years-old. Remi could already feel the excitement in the crisp winter air. 65 and the other orphans were looking forward to visiting the beautiful city of Lux for the New Year festivities, where they'd watch the wealthy citizens celebrate, while praying someone would adopt them this year. The thought sent a shiver racing down Remi's spine. He'd always wanted to be adopted more than anything else in the world, but lately he'd been having second thoughts. He knew his chances of adoption were slim, and getting slimmer with each year older he got. But the chances of someone wanting him *and* 65 were nonexistent. And Remi had recently realized that if adoption meant being separated from his best friend, then he'd rather stay an orphan.

"What?" 65 asked catching Remi's glance. "Do I have dirt on my face?" she whispered looking concerned.

"A little," he said messing with her.

"Where?" she asked, rubbing her cheeks self-consciously.

65 hadn't been marked before, but now she'd done a thorough job of smudging soot from the volcanic ash all over her round freckled cheeks.

"Did I get it?" she asked, her clear-blue eyes as big as saucers.

"Not even close," Remi laughed scurrying over to her. "Here, let me."

"Thanks."

"What would you do without me?" he ribbed playfully when he was done wiping her cheeks with his shirtsleeve.

"Please. You'd be so bored without me," she joked back.

Remi smiled and shook his head as he turned back to his work. He wanted to tell 65 about what he'd just found. He hated keeping things from her. The only secret he'd ever kept from her was that he still remembered his real name – Remi – rather than John #26, the name the Troian Center had unceremoniously given him after the Flood. 65 was so young when she was orphaned that she had no recollection of her name; the one thing she longed for most in the world. It felt selfish of Remi to share that he knew his real name. Not to mention dangerous. He wasn't allowed to use it, so he didn't see the point in sharing. Especially with 65, she had a habit for finding trouble and he didn't want his name to be a source.

65 was Remi's best friend, his only friend. They'd always shared everything. They'd been lumped together as orphans when the Flood stole their families. Being scrawny outcasts they naturally found each other and loneliness made them thick as thieves. Remi was surprised at himself for not instantly skittering over to 65 and showing her the artifact as soon as he'd found it. Maybe it was because he knew she'd make him turn it in, and rightly so. They'd always looked out for each other and keeping something that belonged to Lux was not in Remi's best interest.

The whistle blew while Remi was deep in thought and before he knew it, he was lined up and marching back to the Troian Center with the rest of the eight-year-old orphans. He didn't have time to change his mind. Before he could stop himself, he was smuggling stolen merchandise. The weight of the metal in his pocket taunted him with every step. *Illegal! Stolen! Alert!*

65 reached for his hand and he just about jumped out of his skin. "What's wrong with you?" she whispered.

"What do you mean?"

"I've been talking to you the whole time and you're ignoring me," she said with a pout.

"Oh, sorry. Just lost in thought I guess," Remi replied sheepishly.

"Oh 26, you're lucky I get you."

65 chattered the entire voyage back, filling Remi's mind with idle things and offering a welcome distraction from the heavy guilt lodged in his pocket. He noticed 65 shiver when the wind picked up and he instinctively put his arm around his friend's slender shoulders.

"I hate when it gets cold," Remi whispered.

"I don't mind," 65 replied. "I mean, I prefer the warm weather and all, but when it starts to get cold that means it's getting close to the holidays!"

Remi smirked at his friend's optimism. "But you know we don't get to celebrate the holidays."

"I know, but the locals always get nostalgic and share amazing stories about Father Christmas and gifts wrapped in glittering paper!"

"65..."

"I know, I know. The holidays don't exist anymore because of the stupid Flood. But it's still fun to dream."

"You're right," Remi said as he squeezed her shoulders with melancholy.

His heart panged for his family whenever 65 mentioned the holidays. He, along with the other orphans at the Troian Center had lost their families and friends when a mythical Flood hit their island, devastating over half the population. The only part of the island left untouched was the wealthy city of Lux. Lucky for them a few locals and orphans survived to pick up the pieces. But nothing was the same after that. All the old ways and traditions were taboo now for fear of angering the gods. No one dared risk provoking their wrath. The islanders were so superstitious that they'd even forced the orphans to give up their names for numbers instead thinking it would give them a fresh start and appease the gods.

Remi glanced at 65. She marched steadily beside him, small, yet fierce. Being that he was barely a toddler when he became an orphan, he didn't remember the day he met her exactly, but he knew he couldn't remember a time since the Flood that hadn't been filled with her sparkling blue eyes and dimpled smile. She was his family now and his heart ached knowing that she wouldn't get to celebrate the holidays she dreamed about.

A tiny spark of an idea itched the edges of Remi's mind. He pushed it away as he saw the dark shadow of the Troian Center looming ahead. Some ideas were better left unexplored.

2

When the lights went out Remi went to work. He waited until he heard heavy snores coming from his group bed before he wriggled the lump of steel out of his pocket. In the moonlight the silver metal glowed blue. He huffed on the piece and rubbed it against the cotton of his nightshirt. The pattern finally became clear. He slowly ran his fingers over the etchings that created a beautiful compass rose. He'd read about them, but never seen one in person. It was beautiful and mysterious all at once. While methodically tracing the grooves he heard a faint click and the whirl of gears. Remi cautiously examined the gap where the metal circle had separated, parting into equal pieces. It was an actual compass!

Inside he watched in wonder while the intricate dials sputtered. There were strange nautical markings and references to constellations. It must have come from a ship. He tapped the side of the compass and the needle hiccupped and twitched until finally settling to point directly back at Remi. Compasses are supposed to point North. *The stupid thing must be broken*, he thought. Expecting it not to be had been foolish of course. Not many things had survived the Flood and those that did, weren't what they used to be. That went for people and gadgets alike.

A large boy next to Remi yawned and rolled toward him, almost knocking the compass out of his hand. Remi had to jump out of the way to avoid being flattened by the boy's broad shoulders that were tattooed with the number 22. Remi sighed and tucked the broken compass away for the night. He'd have to find another time to look into it. Preferably when he could see and wasn't being crushed by a snoring orphan.

3

Weeks worth of research and tinkering proved useless. No matter what Remi did, the compass always pointed back to him. It was extremely odd and defied all reason. He tried holding the compass with different hands, from different positions, upside down, right side up, sideways, but no matter what he did the results were always the same. The needle aimed its trembling tip at him. Remi knew it was silly, but he began to think maybe the compass was magic. Perhaps it was bound to whoever unlocked its powers and since that person had been Remi, the compass would always point to him as its true North.

While Remi was pondering this thought during Flood work one day, he caught a sudden movement out of the corner of his eye. It was a large black and white tarcat, swishing its tail while eyeing something inquisitively. Remi followed the direction of its pricked ears and saw that the tarcat's glowing yellow eyes were focused on 65. She was working at the bottom of the rubble pile and the long strings of her shoelaces were untied and trailing behind her. Remi didn't hesitate a moment before springing into action. He scrambled down the rubble pile, sending volcanic debris avalanching behind him. "Shoo! Get out of here! Leave her alone!"

65 spun around just as the angry tarcat hissed and flattened its black ears. Remi pushed himself between them and continued to yell and flail his arms. The tarcat slowly backed away, deciding two targets weren't as enticing prey as one unsuspecting one.

Once the lethal tarcat slinked away, Remi turned to 65. "Are you okay?" he asked breathlessly.

65 looked up at him with her startled blue eyes. She threw her scrawny arms around his waist and squeezed with surprising strength. "Oh my gods! Thank you, 26. I didn't even realize Khan was sneaking up on me. I guess I was lost in my head again."

"You have to pay more attention, 65. And not just to tarcats. To everything," he said.

"That's why I have you. We're in this together. We watch each other's backs. Thick as thieves, remember?" she grinned.

"It might not always be that way," Remi replied with a forlorn look.

"Why not?" she asked suddenly serious. "Are you going somewhere?"

"No, but the New Year Gala is coming up. It's always a possibility."

She scoffed. "Oh, is that what you're worried about? No one wants us, 26."

"Hey! Speak for yourself," he added with mock insult.

"You know I'm not trying to be mean, but look at us. We're the two scrawniest orphans in this place. No one will choose us."

"I hope you're right," Remi mumbled to himself.

Just the thought of being separated from 65 made his heart race. Could she even survive without him there to look out for her? Even though the Troian Center assigned all orphans the same birthday, 65 was almost a year younger than Remi. She was so tiny and thin. Everyone picked on her because she was an easy target and she never knew when to let things go. She was feisty and always stood her ground against the bullies, but it often resulted in injuries and trips to the locker.

But their friendship was balanced. Even though Remi looked out for 65, she was someone he relied on too. He tended to be an observer, which hadn't earned him any friends and if it weren't for 65 he'd have no one to talk to. Plus, she always found a way to cheer him up when he was having a bad day. Her optimism was contagious, making Remi's fears and sadness pale whenever she was around.

65 was right. They were thick as thieves. They needed each other and in the event that they were separated, Remi would have to come up with a plan that would bring them back together.

They continued working the rubble pile in silence. 65 noticed Remi was still staring at her with a distressed look painted across his face. "Stop worrying," she whispered. Then she crossed her eyes and stuck her tongue out to get him to smile.

"Get back to work or we'll both have the locker to worry about," he whispered while fighting a grin.

4

"Guess what I found today?" 65 squealed when she and Remi took their spot at their empty table in the corner of the dining hall.

Remi nearly dropped his fork when she pulled out a wad of shining red paper.

"What is that?" Remi asked as he quickly put his hand over hers to conceal the contraband.

"It's Christmas paper! Can you believe it? One of the locals let me have a piece. He said he'd been collecting what the citizens of Lux discard. Isn't that crazy? Who'd throw this away? It's so pretty!" she said trying to peek through the cracks of Remi's fingers.

"65, you know you can't keep this," he said softly. "We're not allowed to have personal things. If the headmistress finds out you'll get sent to the locker."

65's eyes watered as she stroked the crinkles in the shiny red paper.

"I know. It was just fun to pretend to know what it would be like to get a present from Father Christmas."

"We can pretend in our minds, 65. Anything we imagine can

be true in our dreams," Remi said as he gently pulled the paper from her tiny hands.

He quickly crumpled the paper and concealed it in his pocket before anyone noticed. Luckily no one ever paid attention to their table for outcasts in the corner. He turned back to 65 and gently squeezed her hands. "I promise, one day we'll get out of here and I'll make sure you get a gift from Father Christmas."

65 smiled up at him and sighed. "It's okay. I don't need presents as long as I have you," she said with a slight hiccup.

5

When Remi was getting ready for bed he found the wad of red paper in his pocket. Something stopped him from throwing it away. He knew he was being foolish. He already had one illegal possession. What on earth made him think he could hide two? Whatever it was, he ignored his good sense and slipped the paper into his wardrobe under his socks where he kept the compass and hopped into bed.

That night Remi had the most amazing dream. It was about a pirate ship that moved across the water like a ghost in the night. It looked like it was built of mist and made no noise at all. Glowing mermaids jetted in front of the ship, breaking up the reflection of the stars in the ink black sky as the ship glided on. At the helm was a beautiful witch. Her long grey hair was coiled under a tricorn hat in lumpy braids that fell to her waist. In one hand she gripped the wheel of the ghost ship, in the other she held a shiny brass compass; Remi's compass. "Take me to what I seek most," her haunting voice whispered to Remi's subconscious.

When Remi awoke the idea that had been lightly scratching

the surface of his mind was now a sledgehammer. He knew the compass must be magic. It would take its possessor to the thing they seek most. He had to find a way to give it to 65. That way if they were separated by adoption, she'd always be able to find a way back to him if that's what she sought most. He scratched his head while pondering how he could pull it off. Perhaps he could give her the compass under the guise of a gift from Father Christmas. That way she'd believe it truly had magic. If Remi gave it to her as a relic he'd found in the rubble, she'd just laugh at him and turn it in so they didn't get in trouble. She'd probably be right to do so, but lately Remi had been worrying more and more about being separated from his best friend. The compass must have come to him for this very reason.

He dug through his wardrobe to get dressed; the red glint of the shiny wrapping paper caught his eye. *That's it,* he thought. *I'll wrap it in the Christmas paper and leave it in her sock on Christmas Eve, just like Father Christmas would've.*

Remi whistled a tune with renewed excitement as he got ready for the day. Only two more days until Christmas Eve and he finally had a plan to make it as grand as 65 had always dreamed.

6

"What's gotten into you today?" 65 asked from her perch on the rubble pile. "You've been grinning like you're up to something all day."

"Who, me?" Remi asked unable to hide his smirk.

"You *are* up to something!" she squeaked. "What is it? What is it? You have to let me in on the secret."

"I'm not keeping a secret," Remi replied with his best poker face.

"Oh, please. You're a terrible liar," she said launching a well-aimed attack on his ticklish ribs.

"Mercy! Mercy!" Remi yelled in a fit of laughter.

When 65 relented he seized his chance to tickle her back. She squealed and closed her eyes as she tried to dodge his attack, but in a moment their fun turned to disaster as the pile of debris they stood on shifted, pitching them off balance.

Both Remi and 65 tumbled down the rubble pile, causing a commotion that brought the Grifts and orphans running. It was just minor scrapes and bruises for the most part. The embarrassment and ridicule from the other orphans would be the longest lasting of their injuries. 65 and Remi stood before the Grifts trembling and praying they wouldn't get sent to the locker for horsing around during Flood work.

"What happened here?" a rough looking Grift growled at them.

"Nothing, Sir. The pile just shifted and we fell," Remi said, his eyes turned down.

"What happened to your mouth?"

Remi reached up to feel his fat lip and pulled his hand away quickly as he flinched at the pain.

"Let me see," the Grift grumbled as he gripped Remi's jaw to peer inside his mouth. "You got a loose tooth kid. Let me help ya with it."

Remi cringed but tried not to show it for 65's benefit. She didn't have the stomach for these sorts of things. Even the slightest bit of blood made her squeamish.

The Grift put Remi in a headlock and yanked his tooth out with a sickening pop. Remi tasted blood and spit it to the ground as he fought the urge to cry. He had to be brave for 65. He could already see a torrent of tears streaming down her sooty cheeks.

"Here ya go, kid. Make sure it gets added to yer basket," the Grift said giving Remi a hard pat on the back and turning to yell at the rest of the orphans who were watching instead of working.

Remi grabbed 65's hand and scrambled to the far side of the rubble pile away from the view of the others.

"Are you okay?" he questioned with slurred speech through his swollen lip and sore mouth.

"*Me?* I'm fine. But what about *you*?" she hiccupped. "He ripped your tooth out! This place is the worst!"

"It's alright. It's just a tooth. That one was getting loose anyway," he lied to comfort her. "Look," he said holding it out to her in the palm of his hand.

She delicately took the tiny bone.

"Let's make a wish and bury it," she said, her eyes suddenly hopeful. "Then the fairies will grant it!"

"65, you heard him. It goes in the basket. We can't keep things. Not even our teeth. They fetch a high price at the trade market in Lux."

"It's not fair," she sniveled as Remi took the tooth back and added it to their basket of stones and trinkets they'd collected for Lux. "Just once it would be nice to make a wish."

"What would you wish for?" Remi asked gently.

"I don't know. That's such a tough question. I think I'd wish for a million more wishes," she said with a hint of a twinkle in her eyes. "What would you wish for?"

"That's an easy question for me. I'd wish for you and I to get adopted at the New Year Gala this year by the same loving family so we wouldn't be stuck at the Troian Center anymore."

65's eyes filled with wonder and Remi knew her mind was already imagining what it would be like to have parents, a real home, and to be loved.

7

The day was finally here. Tomorrow was Christmas Eve. Remi could hardly wait to hide 65's gift in her sock. He'd managed to wrap the compass in the scrap of shiny red Christmas paper when everyone was asleep. He planned to sneak it into her wardrobe tonight after lights out. The anticipation was killing him. It seemed like the bell signaling the end of their day would never come.

Remi glanced at 65 for the hundredth time. She was still sitting next to him daydreaming and doodling in her notebook instead of studying for lessons like they were supposed to be. He was about to nudge her when the door to their room opened. Every orphan snapped to attention and got to their feet when they saw who it was. Headmistress Greeley!

Remi's mind reeled and he began to panic. *What was she doing here? Could she know about the compass?*

Greeley peered down at them with disdain and cleared her throat. "It's been brought to my attention that one of you has been keeping something from me. Something that doesn't belong to you," she alleged in her wicked nasally voice.

Remi's heart thundered in his chest. *She knows!*

"Unless the offender comes forward now, you will all suffer the locker."

Remi was about to take a step forward when he saw 65 move. His stomach dropped when she stepped up to Greeley. *What is she doing?*

Remi fought his shock and raced into action. He skidded between Geneva and their headmistress. Greeley's thin eyebrows arched in surprise. "What do we have here? Two offenders?"

"No, it's just me, Headmistress. I'm sorry I kept this from you. It was meant to be a Christmas gift," Remi said as he fished the shiny red package from his pocket.

Greeley's eyes narrowed and she snatched the bundle from Remi's hand. "Disobedience is a disease with you orphans, isn't it? I come looking for one thing and find another. Who has the tooth? Hand it over now!" Greeley thundered and Remi's heart iced over.

No, she wouldn't have...

"I'm sorry," 65 whispered to him as she dug her tiny hand into her pocket and fished out the milky grey tooth. "It was meant to be a Christmas gift, too," she said defiantly to Greeley.

"You will both be severely punished for this. One day for illegal possession, one day for illegal traditions, one day for disobedience and one day foolishness. Your sentence in the Locker starts now."

8

The locker was cold and dark. Remi tried to suppress his shivers, while he rubbed the gooseflesh from his arms.

"I'm sorry I stole your tooth," 65 said.

Remi snorted, unable to contain his laughter at the absurd statement. Soon they were both giggling uncontrollably.

"Yeah, what on earth made you do that?"

"Remember when that local told us that if you bury a tooth and make a wish that a fairy will come from the rainforest and make it come true?"

"Yeah, but that was just a fairytale."

"I know it's stupid, but I just really wanted to give you a wish for Christmas. But I guess we'll be spending Christmas in the locker instead."

"It's not stupid," Remi muttered in the darkness, "You're right, it would've been nice to make a wish that would give us home with a family that loves us. I'm sorry I ruined Christmas, 65."

"You could never ruin Christmas for me. And besides, as long as I'm with you, I am home. We're a family, you and me."

Remi felt his heart swell and he was grateful for the darkness so 65 couldn't see the well of emotions in his eyes. He scooted closer to her so they were side-by-side in the darkness and reached for her hand.

"Thick as thieves," he said lacing his warm fingers with her cold ones.

"Thick as thieves," she replied resting her head on his shoulder.

After a moment, 65 picked her head up. "What was the gift Greeley took from you?" she asked.

"Nothing," Remi replied. "Nothing at all. She actually gave me a gift. I get to spend Christmas with my favorite person in the world."

65 put her head back on Remi's shoulder and began to hum. Together, side-by-side in the darkness, they sang the few verses to the only Christmas song they knew.

"Silent night, holy night!
Gods of magic, gods of light.
Send a savior for peace,
Send a savior for peace."

The Timekeeper's Daughter

A SHORT STORY

C.J. Benjamin

FOREWORD

She could see the future; he could control time.
Their love was forbidden, seen as a crime.
The lovers knew they could not outrace,
Their future was doomed once Death gave chase.
No matter how swift or how clever,
The lovers knew happily ever after wouldn't last forever.

PROLOGUE

There once lived a fairy that was gifted a special
power,
She was more beautiful than even a foxglove flower.
She met a boy with a unique secret of his own,
He could control time, a skill he was desperate
to hone.
Truer love hath never been told,
Yet forces beyond wished them never to behold.
Mother Nature and Father Time met in haste,
To decide what would be their fate.
It was deemed a child of such a union would possess
too much power,
So an army of fairies were sent across the lands
to scour.
Since it was ordered their love should not survive,
The lovers hath no choice but to run for their lives.
They found safety on a little farm off the beaten
path,
But their sanctuary was never meant to last.

1

Arah looked over her shoulder again. She hated when they rode through the woods, but it was the only way to town. She cradled her baby daughter, while keeping an eye on her eldest, sleeping between her and her husband. They all swayed in unison with the moving carriage.

"We're okay," Calen whispered to Arah, giving her shoulders a squeeze. "It's been six years. If they haven't found us by now, they're not going to."

Arah smiled warmly at him. Calen always knew what she was thinking, that was just one of the many things she loved about her husband.

As usual Calen, was right. Their trip to town was uneventful. They traded their crops from the farm and picked up a few more timepieces that needed repair. Arah felt uneasy that word about Calen's skill at repairing watches and clocks had gotten out. She was content to just pose as farmers. But he assured her that it wouldn't raise suspicion because surely a timekeeper on the run wouldn't tinker in his trade. He called it hiding in plain sight.

Calen was a timekeeper. He could control time at his

leisure, turning it back, slowing it down, jumping ahead or freezing it completely. But that wasn't why they were in hiding. There were many timekeepers in the world. They worked for Father Time and did his bidding; repairing holes in time, thwarting time travelers who didn't pay their tolls, mending the ripple effect from unfortunate events the governing gods decided to erase. Timekeepers were necessary and they never abused their powers. The problem arose when a timekeeper married a fairy. And not just any fairy; one who could see the future.

Arah felt she was to blame for their life on the run. She was Fae born and possessed a special gift. She was a todhchaí, which meant she could see the future. This made her very valuable to the Fae. They wooed her and showered her with gifts, teaching her how to use her power. The Fairy Queen was pleased with her skills. Arah's gift was remarkable. Everything she foretold came true with astounding accuracy. Never had the gift of todhchai been so strong in another.

The Fairy Queen invited Arah to come live with her in the Fae court, where together they would use her powers to rule. But when Arah looked into her future she saw two paths. One led to the Queen's court, where her powers would be exploited for the Queen's own gain and many would suffer. The other led to a handsome man. He was kind and loyal, and surrounded by travel and mystery.

Arah chose to turn down the Queen's offer and follow the second path. She knew the Queen wouldn't take no for an answer, so Arah snuck away, like a shadow into the night, planning never to return. She met Calen the next day. When their eyes fell upon each other she instantly knew he was the one. She fell in love with him the moment they met. He felt the same and vowed to always protect her. They ran away together and wed in secret. That's when their problems began.

While in hiding, Arah had two beautiful daughters. But

shortly after their births, she started to have dark visions. She saw that the Fairy Queen and Father Time were angry and feared the powers that her daughters would one day grow to possess. An army of Fae were sent after them. Arah, Calen and their daughters had been on the run ever since. The tiny farmhouse on Hullabee Island was the longest they'd spent in any one place since the children were born. Despite the constant uneasy feeling Arah had, she was doing her best to try to be happy here. She knew Calen liked being a farmer and tinkering with his clocks. And it seemed a peaceful place to raise her children.

Her eldest daughter had already made friends with some of the local children. A little boy from the native tribe followed her around like a lost puppy. In the short time they'd lived on Hullabee Island, the two children had become inseparable. It warmed Arah's heart to see her daughter make a friend. She wanted her to have a chance at a normal childhood. That notion alone made Arah fight her instincts to run. She loved to watch her daughter and her little friend play together on the farm. They spent hours helping Calen tinker with his clocks, earning her daughter the nickname Tink from the little boy. He would bring her wild flowers from the forest and she would give him fruit from the farm. They couldn't be more different – he with is dark skin and black hair, she with her freckles and strawberry blonde pigtails. Yet they were kindred spirits. They even shared similar names – Mala and Mali.

2

One lazy afternoon, while riding back from town, something changed. Arah felt the change in the air and it sparked her visions. She clutched at Calen's arm and he pulled up the horses.

"Arah, what is it?" he asked.

"Darkness," Arah said quivering.

"Let me get you home," he soothed.

As Calen angled the carriage toward the farm, a dark figure came into view at the top of the hill. He wore a long black hooded cloak and walked with a staff. Arah's hair stood on end when she saw him. She wrapped her hand around Calen's arm in fear and he gave her an understanding glance. He was the darkness she had sensed. Calen slowed the horses as they approached the figure.

"Can I help you, sir?" Calen questioned.

"Yes, I hope you can. I have a broken clock, of sorts, and was kindly directed to this farm."

"Well you're in the right place. This is my farm and I repair timepieces here."

"I have a rather unique piece that I need you to repair," said the cloaked man, handing Calen a heavy metal piece on a chain. He examined it, turning it over in his hand. It was silver with intricate carvings on the front.

"This is a compass," Calen said. "I'm afraid I don't know how to fix it. I only work with timepieces."

"It's a very special compass," the man said. "It means the world to me. I've taken it to dozens of clockmakers and no one can seem to fix it."

"Then what makes you think I can?" Calen asked.

"Well," he whispered. "I've heard you're special. Just like my compass. You see, when it's working, its arrow points to what I most desire. In my line of work it's very important. It helps me find people when the time is right."

Arah squeezed Calen's arm, fearing this man knew their secret. The man smiled at the fear in her blue eyes and let his hood drop causing her to scream. She knew his face immediately. It was the face she'd seen in every vision where someone died. The man who stood before her, was Death, himself. She knew he would come for her someday, but now that she stared Death in the face she was frozen in fear. They'd been found at last.

"Please," she begged. "You can take me, but spare my daughters. I can't let them pay for my crimes. They're just children. They've done nothing wrong. And neither has my husband. His only crime is loving me."

"Relax my dear. It is true I know who you are, but it is as I've said. I'm here for your husband's services."

"So you'll let us live?" she asked in confusion.

Death smiled cruelly and scratched his boney chin. "You would fetch quite a fee, it's true" he said jingling a purse of coins. "But, I already have more coin than I can ever spend and I'm not an unreasonable man. I'll make you a deal," Death said. "If you can fix my compass, I'll wipe you from the great book while letting you keep your lives."

"The great book?" Calen asked.

"Yes, it keeps a list of who is alive and where. Once your name is stricken from its records you will no longer be hunted."

Arah looked at her husband. This deal seemed too good to be true.

"Is it agreed?" Death asked, extending his long, skeletal arm.

"Agreed," Calen said taking it.

Death smiled. "You have one week," he said.

And with that, he slammed his staff into the dirt. His black cloak swirled about him, folding in on itself, until a large black raven emerged. It flew away, leaving them with the echoes of its caws, sounding like laughter in the wind.

3

Calen worked on the compass tirelessly, but to no avail. The compass needle never moved. Not one quiver, dance or sway. Arah and Calen grew desperate as their time grew short.

"This isn't working. It must have been a trick. We need to run, Calen," Arah begged.

"Arah," he groaned. "We can't outrun Death."

"Then let me talk to the fairies," she pleaded.

"No! Arah, we agreed it's too dangerous."

"Calen! Death has already found us. It can't get much worse! Besides, maybe the Fae will help us. Maybe I can make a deal with them," Arah begged.

"You know you can't trust them," Calen replied. "Just give me some more time. If I can fix this compass we'll be safe. With Death on our side, we'll never have to run again. Please, Arah. Have faith in me. I love you. I won't let anything happen to you or our daughters."

~

"Why are you and Father sad?" Mala asked when Arah stormed out of Calen's workshop.

"We're not sad, angel. Your father is just very busy. He's working on fixing a very special clock for a very important man."

"Maybe I can help him," Mala chirped.

"I wish you could, baby," Arah said pulling her daughter into her arms. "I love you very much. You know that, right?"

"Yes, Mother."

"Okay, good girl. Would you like to come for a walk with me?"

"Yes! Can Mali come?" Mala asked.

"Not this time. But your sister can come. Let's go get her."

Together, Arah and her girls went for a walk in the woods – her baby in her arms and Mala underfoot. They wandered until they came upon a patch of beautiful pink flowers.

"These are the most beautiful flowers I've ever seen Mother," Mala crooned.

"These are called Foxglove. They're very special flowers. Do you see how the petals look like tiny bells?" Arah asked.

Mala nodded.

"Well that's because they serve as homes for the fairies."

"Fairies live in there?" Mala asked, her blue eyes growing larger.

"Yes." Arah smiled. "And if I ask really nicely the fairies will let me use some of their magic to see something special."

"What?"

"The future."

Mala watched while her mother whispered into the petals. After a moment, she plucked a pink flower from its stem. She closed her eyes and shook the bell shaped bloom over her face. The pollen that cascaded from the flower mesmerized Mala. It shimmered and danced in the sunlight as it floated in the heavy forest air before landing delicately on her mother's face.

When Arah opened her eyes, they were filled with tears. “Not my daughters” she whispered. “Take me instead.”

“Mother, what’s wrong?” Mala asked.

“Nothing, angel. Let’s go home.” Arah, scooped up her daughters and ran all the way back to the farm.

4

That night Mala listened to her parents fight. Her mother cried as she threw clothes into a trunk just as quickly as her father pulled them out. Mala hated seeing her parents upset. She thought perhaps if she could fix the special clock they would be happy again. She tiptoed out of bed and scurried out her window. She snuck quietly into her father's shop and found the special clock. Her mother was right; it must be very special indeed. It looked like no other clock she'd ever seen before. The heavy silver piece was on a long thick chain. And its face was carved with an eight-pointed star.

Mala traced her fingers over the beautiful design. There were dozens of dots and dashes in a circle around the star. She wondered what it meant. As she ran her small fingers around the edge she heard a click and the clock split in half! Mala slowly opened it and gazed at the delicate needle that sat in the center. She'd never seen something so intriguing before. No wonder her father couldn't fix it. This wasn't a clock at all, of that she was sure. But she had no idea what it was. She wondered if her friend Mali might know. He knew all kinds of things. He taught her about plants and animals and stars. He was full of ideas.

Mala slipped the strange clock into her pocket and decided she would find Mali and ask him about it. She was going to wait until morning, but when she crept back toward the house she could still hear her parents fighting. "We have to leave, now!" her mother cried. Mala's heart sank. She didn't want to leave another home. She loved it here. And she had a best friend. She decided there was no time to waste. She swallowed her fear and ran toward the forest in search of her friend.

Mala knew just where to look. She found Mali sleeping in his family's treetop home deep within the forest. She followed the glowing markers just as he'd taught her. She made the call of an owl, hooting three times. That was always their signal when they wanted to meet. Sure enough, Mali's head popped up from the branches. Mala waved to him and he smiled back at her, white teeth gleaming in the moonlight.

When he came down to meet her, she wasted no time showing him the clock.

"Mala, I wish I could help, but I have no idea what this is. I've never seen it before. What was so important about it that you came all the way out here at night?"

Mala shared her dilemma. "A strange man asked my father to fix it and if he can't I think something bad will happen."

"What makes you say that?"

"My mother went to speak to the fairies today. She asked them for help and to let her see the future. It made her cry and we ran all the way home. I don't know what she saw but when she told my father he got mad. They've been fighting all night and my mother keeps packing our things into a trunk. I think she's going to make us move away."

"You can't! You're my best friend," Mali cried.

"I don't want to leave," Mala said. "But I don't know what to do."

"We have to fix this clock so you don't have to go away."

"But I don't know how. I'm not even sure it's a clock at all."

"You said your mother asked the fairies for help? Do you think the fairies would help you with the clock?" he asked.

"There's only one way to find out."

5

Mala led the way back to the place where her mother brought her. The fairy grove looked even more beautiful at night. The whole area glowed as lava pixies danced above the pink petals, making them shimmer in their effervescent glow. They crept through the moonlight and knelt down among the bell shaped flowers.

"So the fairies live in here?" Mali whispered.

Mala nodded.

"What do we do?" he asked.

"We ask them for help," Mala replied. "Mother said when she asks nicely the fairies let her use their magic."

"So ask if they'll use their magic to fix the clock."

"Okay," Mala said nervously. She leaned in close to the nearest petal and whispered. "Dear fairies, may I borrow some of your magic to fix this special clock for my parents?"

Mali nodded his approval.

Suddenly a fierce wind picked up, causing them to huddle together. When they turned back to the flowers, they were glowing! Tiny orbs of light floated out of the petals. They made a noise that sounded like the chiming of bells. The ringing grew louder and merged together to shape a single voice. "My heated wills encumber, who dare disturb the fairies slumber?"

"Um, I'm sorry, your fairyness. I didn't mean to wake you," Mala replied nervously.

"You are but a child?" the twinkling voice asked. "Alone in the wild?"

"Yes, it's just my friend and I," Mala replied.

"The wood is not safe at night. There are things here that might cause quite a fright."

"We're sorry to bother you, we'll be on our way," Mali said tugging at Mala's arm.

"But I didn't get to ask my question," Mala argued as he pulled her away.

The glowing light surged and circled around them, trapping them with a pealing glow. "Not so quickly fair children, I'm already awake. Ask me your question, how long can it take?" the voice inquired.

"I have a special clock that I need to help my father fix. If it stays broken I think I have to move away again," Mala said. "My mother came here because you can show her the future. Can you look into the future to see if there's a way we can fix this clock?"

"Ah, The future is fickle, my dear. But nevertheless, show me the clock, child, if it's the future you fear."

Mala pulled the timepiece from her pocket. The glowing light surrounded it, twinkling with excitement. "Very special indeed," rang the voice. "I can fix this clock, if that's what you need."

"You can?" Mala asked eagerly.

"But of course, child. It is but a simple task. You need to do nothing more than ask."

Mala and Mali exchanged looks. Mali shrugged and Mala turned back to the light. "Please fix my clock your fairyness," she said.

"As you wish."

After the twinkling voice spoke the words, the wind swirled suddenly about again, causing the pink flowers to quake. Their glittering pollen floated high into the air, swirling in the gale. Mala squealed as the clock yanked itself from her grip and joined the pollen in its aerial dance. The timepiece clicked open and exploded into hundreds of parts. Tiny silver gears in all different sizes and shapes glistened above Mala's head. She watched in awe as glowing lava pixies joined the dance, maneuvering the gears over and over, in a fluid waltz until they wove the timepiece seamlessly back together again.

Just as abruptly as the squall began, it dissipated. And the clock dropped gently back into Mala's hand while the pollen rained down upon her and Mali, kissing their cheeks and spattering their hair. Mala opened the strange clock and stared in wonder. There was a faint whirling sound as the single dial that had been broken, now spun rapidly with ease.

"It works," she whispered.

The voice returned, thundering through the sleeping forest. "Was there ever any doubt? The word of a fairy carries much clout."

"Thank you, your fairyness," Mala said. "You fixed the clock. My family will be so happy! I'm so very grateful to you."

"Dear child, the pleasure was mine. Now what gifts have you for me to pine?"

Mala and Mali exchanged worried glances. "We have no gifts," Mala said.

"Well that doesn't seem fair. I must get something in return to be square."

"But we have nothing to give," Mali pleaded.

The voice shook the forest. "A gift I bestowed, a gift I am owed!"

Mali grabbed Mala's hand. They were too frightened to move and waited for the voice to continue.

"Oh there, there. Do not despair. Mortals always have a gift to give. Let us strike a deal so you may see I am willing to forgive. As long as you deliver one, our transaction shall be done."

"What do you want from us?" Mala asked.

"Did you know fairies trade magic for secrets?" the voice whispered. "I gave your old watch life with my magic. Now you must tell me a secret that's tragic."

"I don't know what that means," Mala whimpered.

"I can think of one such secret for you to give. Tell me child, where is it that you live?"

"On a farm on top of a hill. It's very near here," Mala replied.

"How pleasing to hear. You best run along now, I wouldn't want your parents to fear."

"Thank you," Mala called as she and Mali left the shimmering fairy grove. She couldn't believer her luck! She had trouble keeping the skip from her step as she ran back to her home, listening to the whirl of strange silver clock in her hand.

6

Mala's home came into view just as dawn broke the horizon. She and Mali gazed up the hill to her home and instantly knew something was wrong. A large plume of smoke billowed from the rooftop. Panic raced through Mala's heart as she and Mali ran toward her house.

The house was in shambles. Windows were broken, the thatch roof smoldered and Mala's father lay unconscious on the ground. Mala skittered to stop next to him, shaking him and calling his name to no avail. The wails of her baby sister rang out from inside the smoking house. "My sister!" Mala cried.

"Stay here," Mali ordered.

He raced into the house. Moments later he returned with a baby cradled in his arms. Mala let out a sigh of relief as she gathered her sister in her arms. "Where's my mother? Was she not inside?"

"There was no one else inside," Mali said.

Mala stroked her father's head and called his name. "Father! Father! What happened? Where's Mother? Father, please!" she cried. "I fixed your clock. Everything is supposed to be better now."

Finally her father came to, sputtering and gasping for air.

"Father!" Mala cried. "What happened? Where's Mother?"

His throat was too dry to speak, but he waved a shred of paper clutched in his bruised hand. Mala gently eased it from his clenched fingers. She unfolded it and looked at the single sentence scrawled in beautiful penmanship.

The debt has been paid.

EPILOGUE

Days passed slowly and still Mala's mother didn't return. Mala told her father exactly what happened with the fairies in the forest. They retraced her steps each day but it was no use. The fairy grove had vanished.

Soon Death returned to collect his clock. He was very pleased to see it was working again. He made good on his word to erase Calen and his daughters from the great book. But alas, there was nothing to be done for Arah. It seemed that the Fae had claimed her. And they were outside the realm of even Death.

TIME PASSED. Days faded into months, months to years. Mala and Mali filled that time with each other. Their implausible night in the forest cemented their friendship even further. Mali spent more and more time with Mala and her family helping however he could. Mala found herself filling the role of mother to her little sister. It broke her heart to hear her cry out for their mother daily.

"Do you think she'll ever come back?" Mala asked Mali one day.

"We mustn't give up hope," he said comfortingly.

He pulled her into his embrace and they held each other in silence for a short moment before the cries of Mala's sister pulled them apart.

"This is all my fault," Mala whispered. "She cries all the time and I don't know how to soothe her. She doesn't understand why our mother is gone. Every time she says Mommy it tears my heart to shreds all over again."

"Come on. I'll help you with her," Mali said. "Maybe we can take her to your father's shop. That always made you smile, Tink."

"Mali, please don't call me that anymore. If I didn't meddle in things I didn't understand, none of this would have happened," Mala said sadly.

She left Mali alone to tend to her sister.

When Mala entered her sister's room, she found her standing in her crib as turrets of water poured from it. Her tears streamed steadily, flowing into an impossible deluge of water.

Mala lunged into action, running through the ankle deep water. Her sister shrieked louder, reaching her hands up, begging Mala to pick her up and rescue her from the flood. Mala grabbed her, but as soon as her tiny arms were around her neck a massive tremor shook the house and a searing pain tore through Mala's mind. She closed her eyes tightly as images rapidly flashed through her mind – Fire, Water, Wind, Earth! All the elements in turmoil. Their island destroyed by a catastrophic storm that had never been seen before. The images vanished as quickly as they'd appeared, leaving Mala and her sister in silence in the sopping wet room.

Mala stared into her sister's bright blue eyes. They blinked curiously back at her; long lashes stuck together with tears, but she was no longer crying. Mala hugged her tight anyway, stroking her damp auburn hair. “It’s going to be okay,” Mala soothed. “I won’t let anything happen to you. I promise, Sadie.”

The Floating Stone

A SHORT STORY

C.J. Benjamin

FOREWORD

The Marauded Mariner's Hymn

Gods of sea and gods of light,
Let me be another night.

Up and down the ravaged shore,
Let me seek my love once more.

Among the debris lay things so still,
Things that make me pale and ill.

What is stone and what is bone?
The sea hisses and howls, I am alone.

But waves and peril will not shake my hope,
My love is stronger than a hangman's rope.

Despite the call from briny throats.
I never forget it is hope that floats.

PROLOGUE

There once lived a mermaid who longed to leave
her clan.
All because she fell in love with a mortal, a
simple man.

On a day such as this, a violent storm sprung from
the sea.
The man's vessel tried to outrun it, but alas it was
not meant to be.

His ship and crew sunk to the ocean floor.
The man struggled until he could no more.

The mermaid saw the light fading from his soft
brown eyes.
She knew she was forbidden to interfere, but she was
very wise.

She picked up a white porous stone and filled it
with air.

She infused it with a wish, her heart's honest prayer.

Full of such selfless love, the airy stone began to float.
It pulled the man to the surface where he would be rescued by boat.

Ever since that day, the mermaid and the man were connected.
Forever separated by the sea and the land, a plan they erected.

They could only communicate through their magic white stone.
They would fill it with secrets and wishes of how their love had grown.

But too soon the man grew tired of being apart.
His words were heavy and full of sorrow, like his heart.

When the stone sunk full of sadness the mermaid was quick to forgive.
She filled the stone with hope, so it would float back to him, reminding him to live.

It went on like this for a while until the man could take it no more.
To the mermaid's dismay he traded her hope for the ocean floor.

Let this be a lesson, from which you take note.
Never give up on hope, for hope will always float.

1

Sparrow rolled the pale white stone through her fingers. It always reminded her of the day she found Journey, lying in a lifeless heap on the beach. He was the first person she'd met after the Flood—and he hadn't left her side since. She glanced over at him working next to her. He was effortlessly sorting through large stones on the rubble pile. When he turned just right, sunlight caught his amber eyes, lighting them up like flames. Every time she saw the light behind his eyes she said a silent prayer, thanking the magic white stone that had brought him to her. She bit her lip as the memories hit her with a freshness not thwarted by time.

THE FIRST TIME Sparrow saw Journey, he was lying in the surf. Crashing waves tumbled him to shore. Seeing the movement her heart skipped a beat. She'd found someone who was alive! Thinking he was in need of help, Sparrow ran to him. But when she arrived it was apparent he was just another body washed ashore from the Flood. Her heart tore. He was just a boy—likely the same age as she. He didn't deserve to die this way. No one did. Sparrow knelt down and laid her tiny hands on the boy. He was so cold. She pulled him with all her might, until she dragged him far enough away from the water.

Exhausted and overwhelmed with sadness, Sparrow collapsed. She couldn't take it anymore. Her entire life had changed in one day. The last thing she remembered was her mother clinging to her in a boat as the torrents of water rushed through their village. Then she awoke, alone on the shore, surrounded by people who weren't moving. She searched every one of them. None were alive. And none were her mother.

Finding the lifeless boy in the surf had been more than Sparrow could handle. Convinced she'd be alone forever, Sparrow began to cry. She squeezed the cold hands of the motionless boy, crying harder and harder, wishing there was something she could do. Anything to help the victims of the Flood that lay scattered on the beach—anything to bring them back.

Suddenly, Sparrow felt the hands she was holding squeeze back. She gasped in awe as the boy sputtered and choked. Sparrow sprung into action and quickly rolled him onto his side as he coughed up half the ocean, including one tiny white pebble. When Sparrow saw the stone, she knew exactly what it was—a floating stone! A stone full of magic and hope. A stone that granted wishes. Her mother had told her the fairytale about the mermaid and the man a thousand times. Perhaps her mother was waiting for Sparrow in the glittering city under the sea. Maybe she sent Sparrow this boy and the stone to help her until they could be together again.

Those hopeful thoughts caused Sparrow to cling to the stone as though her life depended on it. She carried it with her everywhere, convinced any good fortune that came her way was because of the magic stone.

SPARROW GAZED from the tiny white stone she held in her hand to where Journey was sorting rubble nearby. She smiled at the fond memories of how her floating stone had brought Journey to her.

2

The day Sparrow found Journey on the beach was the first time she ever healed anyone. Of course she didn't know she could do magic at the time. After all she was just a child back then. She attributed the magical miracle to the floating stone Journey had coughed up. Sparrow had no idea what real magic was, or that she could use it to heal people. She also had no idea that the boy she rescued would become her best friend, her protector, her shadow, her everything. His name was Journey and he seemed to think since she'd saved his life, he was indebted to her service.

A million times since that fateful day, Sparrow told Journey that he didn't owe her anything. Besides, he'd returned the favor of saving her live time and time again. She was convinced she would have never made it off the beach if it weren't for Journey. He was the one who knew how to survive. He built a shelter by thatching the palms together. He found coconuts and showed her how to drink from them and eat the sweet white flesh inside. He kept her warm every night when the angry winds howled off the sea. And he kept her safe from the predators that lurked the shore each night, scavenging the remains of the Flood.

Sparrow and Journey had been stranded for two whole weeks before they were found and brought to the Troian Center. During that entire time, Journey had only said two things to Sparrow. After coughing up the sea, he caught his breath and told her his name and thanked her for rescuing him. Sparrow launched herself at him, wrapping her arms around him in an ecstatic hug. She was so unbelievable happy to no longer be alone. Not to mention she was convinced the floating stone had brought Journey to her for a reason. When she told him so, he merely smirked and laughed off the idea. It frustrated Sparrow to no end that Journey didn't believe in the magic of the stone. She was always trying to prove its powers to him.

She filled their idle time by chattered to him nonstop. Looking back, she wondered if her incessant blathering had bothered him, since he rarely had use for words himself. But it seemed Journey enjoyed her company, because he never left her side. And, when the Grifts brought them to the Troian Center and tried to separate them, he found words. Fierce words that still echoed through Sparrow's mind.

"She is my family! If you try to keep us apart, it will be the last thing you ever attempt."

3

Journey had told the Grifts Sparrow was his twin sister and he would kill anyone who tried to keep them apart. Of course, it was blatantly obvious they weren't twins. Despite sharing the same shade of tawny brown hair and light amber eyes, Sparrow and Journey couldn't look more different. Journey towered over her. He was definitely older and built like a stone—muscular and solid. Sparrow on the other hand seemed constructed of hollow bones. She was all limbs—lanky, boney and fragile.

Journey's fabricated story of twins didn't fly, but his persistence in escaping his room to return to Sparrow's every chance he got wore the Grifts down. Eventually, they decided to accept his tale, and Journey and Sparrow were allowed to bunk together as long as they would follow the rules of their new lives at the Troian Center. This new life entailed leaving their names behind. Journey became John #22 and Sparrow became Jane #42. Both bore bold tattoos on their shoulders to remind them of their new identities; or lack there of. But they both accepted their new lives and had never been separated since.

Sparrow remembered the first night that Journey had been

allowed to join the rest of the children in her room. She was crowded in the tiny straw cot with her bunkmates, sharing a single sparse blanket among them. But Journey avoided the cot and moved to the corner of the room to sit under the window. Sparrow watched as he made himself comfortable and rested his head against the wall. She thought perhaps he felt like an outcast among the unfamiliar children, so she crawled out of bed to join him.

This became their routine. Each night they would sleep under the window, bathed in the moonlight that filtered in. Sparrow would curl up under Journey's warm arm, just as she'd done during their time on the beach. No one complained. The other orphans were happy for more room in their bed and the Grifts were happy as long as the children kept quiet and stayed in their room.

4

One particularly cold night, Sparrow couldn't fall asleep. She shivered against Journey unable to get warm. He took off his threadbare shirt and offered it to her.

"But you'll be cold," she whispered as he draped it over her thin shoulders.

Journey shook his head and pulled her under his arm again.

"Are you going to sleep over here every night?" Sparrow asked.

He nodded.

"Why?"

Journey was silent for so long Sparrow thought this would just be another question left unanswered. He wasn't one for talking. She'd learned to ask yes or no questions most of the time if she wanted a response from him.

So Sparrow was startled when a voice softly rumbled through the chest she leaned against. "To keep you safe," Journey murmured.

Sparrow gazed up at his moonlit eyes. "What do you mean?"

Journey sighed. These weren't questions he could answer with one word and Sparrow knew that vexed him.

"I can protect you better here."

"But we're safe at the Troian Center," Sparrow replied.

"We're orphans," Journey answered. "We're never safe."

Sparrow hated seeing the worry that filled his amber eyes. She pulled her tiny white stone out of her pocket and placed it in his hand. "You don't have to worry. We have this," she said.

Journey shook his head.

"I know you don't believe in the floating stone's magic, but I do," she whispered.

He stared blankly at the weightless pebble.

"It's taken care of us so far. How can you not believe in its power?"

He shrugged.

Sparrow's eyes grew teary. The floating stone was one of her favorite tales. Her mother used to tell it to her nearly every night before bed. Though she'd shared the tale with Journey many times before, she snuggled in closer to tell him the story again. "A long time ago there was a mermaid and man who fell in love. They longed for a way they could be together. They had a special stone that would carry their messages back and forth to each other. It was white and airy like this stone," she said pointing to the stone now in his hand. "It's so light so they could fill it with hope and it would carry their messages of love. And since hope floats, the stone would float from the man to the mermaid and the mermaid to the man."

Journey smiled at Sparrow, waiting for the story to continue.

"But one day the man had no hope to fill the stone with. He was sad and tired of living apart from the mermaid. When he sent the stone into the sea it sank because the man had lost hope. The mermaid searched everywhere but she couldn't find their special stone. It had fallen to the bottom of the sea with all the other lost hopes and dreams. Without it, they couldn't communicate and the man grew so desperate that he threw himself into the sea to be with the mermaid one last time before he sunk to the hopeless ocean floor."

Journey stared at her with skepticism.

"You can think it's a fairytale all you want," Sparrow whispered. "But the moral of the story applies whether you believe in the floating stone or not. Don't give up hope, Journey. Without it we have nothing."

"We have each other," he replied giving her shoulders a squeeze.

"Exactly. And we have the floating stone to thank for that."

Journey smirked and shook his head, as he always did when he thought Sparrow was being silly.

"I know this stone is magic. When I found you I wished there was something I could do to help you and you came to life! You were choking on this very stone!"

Journey's expression changed. He looked back at the porous stone, rolling it around between his fingers and thumb.

Sparrow continued. "When we were trying to survive on the beach, I wished someone would rescue us. And they did. And when we arrived here, I wished for a way we could stay together. And we have. Now I wish for us to be safe. And we are."

Sparrow put her small hand in Journey's large one. "I've been filling this stone with hope and it's granted all of my wishes. We'll be safe as long as we have it," she said. "It's magic, Journey. You just have to believe in it."

Journey placed the stone in Sparrow's hand and leaned back against the wall. "Magic doesn't exist anymore," he replied. Then he shut his eyes.

5

Over the years Sparrow began to think Journey was right. After the Flood, the magic that had once made their island a beautiful and enchanting place seemed to have vanished. Sparrow had been wrong to assume they were safe at the Troian Center. She began to see their new home for what it really was a prison work camp for orphans.

They spent their days slaving away doing the manual labor it took to run a place filled with orphans. Sparrow grew pale from all the time she spent confined indoors. She was always doing laundry, scrubbing floors or working over the hot fires of the kitchen. Her only salvation was that wherever she was, Journey was right there with her.

Journey always managed to make Sparrow smile, even without words—the slight arch of his eyebrows when one of the other orphans would talk back to a Grift, or his quick smirks when he used his menacing physique to get the other orphans to leave them alone. That's why, when Journey was assigned to Flood work without her, Sparrow was completely distraught.

It was obvious Journey's strength and size would be an asset to working the rubble piles rather than sorting laundry. It was a miracle it'd taken so long for the Grifts to realize his physicality was being wasted in the laundry room. Still, it came as a shock to them both. They'd never been separated before. To say Journey didn't take the news well was an understatement. He fought the Grifts with untamed fury, kicking biting, and wrestling—anything to delay the inevitable. But each day, the Grifts outlasted Journey and beat him into submission so they could drag him to the fields for Flood work.

It broke Sparrow's heart to see Journey treated this way. Every night she would wish on her floating stone for Journey's safety while tending to his wounds under the pale moonlight that filtered in through the windows in their bunkroom. She begged Journey to go to Flood work willingly because she couldn't bear to see him treated this way. But he would just shake his head and reply, "I have to keep you safe."

"Wish on the stone with me," Sparrow pleaded. "Wish that tomorrow will bring us to a better place."

But Journey never wished. He would only hug Sparrow to him and say, "I'm already in the best place I could be, by your side."

6

Journey's resistance got so bad that one day he didn't return from Flood work. When he didn't show up for dinner, Sparrow frantically searched the crowd of orphans in the dining hall. But Journey wasn't among them. Journey was never one to miss a meal. Her heart began to tremble with worry. Sparrow made her way around the room, table by table, asking if anyone knew where Journey was.

Everyone ignored her. The older orphans Journey had been assigned to Flood work with didn't associate with lowly Janes like herself. But Sparrow didn't care. She pestered each of them until she found what she was looking for. Answers.

Sparrow finally came upon a kind faced boy with green eyes and wavy gold hair. He took pity on her and invited her to sit down.

"Have you seen my friend?" she asked. "His name is John #22 and he hasn't returned from Flood work today."

The boy's green eyes sparkled while he pondered her question. Sparrow's cheeks burned when she met his emerald green eyes, so she stared at his tattoo instead while waiting for his answer. The bold Roman numeral XVIII stared back at her.

"Your friend tried to escape today," the boy whispered.

"What?" Sparrow gasped in astonishment. *Journey would never leave her.*

"Relax, he wasn't running away. The big lug was actually running back toward the Troian Center."

Sparrow stared at the fetching green-eyed boy in confusion. He answered her question, but she didn't remember actually asking it. He seemed to catch her bewilderment and gave her a wink. This only confused her further, but she shook her head, focusing on her main concern. "Where is he?"

"Rumor is, the Locker."

A shiver ran down Sparrow's spine. The Locker was the worst place in the world. Everyone was sent there once to experience its horrors so that later the mere threat of it was enough to keep even the most petulant child in line.

Sparrow hated the thought of Journey spending his night in the pitch black hole under the stone floor of the Troian Center. It was cold and wet and there were definitely creepy crawly things lurking in the darkness. *Why couldn't he just be reasonable?* Sparrow was livid. She was fine on her own. She could look after herself while Journey was at Flood work.

7

But it seemed Journey was right, yet again. Sparrow wasn't safe without him. As his accommodations in the Locker became a permanent thing the other orphans noticed his absence and began to target her. The Johns stole her food and the Janes taunted and teased her. They called her names like scrawny bird or little leech. Without Journey's menacing demeanor to keep the other orphans at bay, Sparrow became easy prey.

They wouldn't even let her back in the oversized group bed.

"You think just because your lap dog is gone we're going to take you back?" a girl with vicious black eyes sneered. "Find someone else to keep you warm," she said shoving Sparrow away from the bed.

"Oh John 22, where are you. I miss you giant arms around me," the Janes mocked from their bed, while Sparrow sobbed silently in the corner.

Sparrow balled herself up tightly beneath the window and pulled out her floating stone. She filled it with all the hope she had left and wished with all of her might for Journey to come back to her and for things to get better.

8

The next day Sparrow was assigned laundry duty again. She kept to herself while scrubbing the filthy uniforms of the other orphans. The Janes working with her that day were particularly vile. A pretty Jane, with long black hair to the middle of her back was currently picking on a smaller girl with white blonde curls.

"Are you going to cry again, Jane 65?" called the girl with the raven black hair. "Are you sad because you have no friends and you're all alone?" she taunted.

"I ha-ha-have friends," 65 replied bravely.

The other Janes cackled as the tiny blonde girl stuttered over her words.

Sparrow hated herself for standing by and watching the other Janes torment Jane 65, who'd done nothing to provoke their foul behavior. She was merely small, therefore an easy target. That was the way things were at the Troian Center. The strong picked on the weak. And for the first time Sparrow was realizing, without Journey, she was weak. He had always been there—a fixture in her life. Almost functioning like another appendage, and now that he was gone it was like her right arm had been lopped off and she was at a loss for how to function without it.

Sparrow was shaking with anger. She wished there was something she could do to help the bullied girl as she listened to the older Janes sing the haunting words of a sad old mariner's hymn.

"What is stone and what is bone? The sea hisses and howls, and you're all alone."

They repeated that line over and over, pushing the smaller Jane and laughing. Sparrow hated that song. She heard the locals singing it often enough to know it was a terrible song about death.

"Those aren't even the right words," the smaller girl yelled, pushing back.

The black-haired girl hissed. "What did you say to me?"

"I said— "

But a loud *slap* interrupted the rest of her response. Sparrow whipped around, no longer able to keep quiet. She knew she was sealing her fate but she couldn't stand by and watch them beat this poor girl.

"Leave her alone!" Sparrow yelled.

"Oh look, maybe she does have a friend after all," the black-haired girl purred as she slinked toward Sparrow with deadly intent.

Sparrow closed her fingers around the tiny white stone in her pocket as the black-haired girl approached and silently prayed to the gods for help. *Please grant my wish. Please take me away from here!*

"What's in your pocket?" The black-haired girl asked.

"Nothing," Sparrow replied, clamping her fist closed around her stone.

"She's got something!" And like that the other Jane's were upon her, pulling the stone from Sparrow's hand.

"No!" Sparrow screamed as they pried the stone from her grasp.

Just then the door to the laundry room creaked open and the headmistress loomed over them.

"What in the name of the gods is going on in here?"

The girls all scrambled to their feet to present themselves to their headmistress. She was notorious for her quick temper and swift punishment. Sparrow stood straight as an arrow and looked at her dirty feet, too petrified to meet the headmistress's glare.

"I asked a question!" the headmistress yelled, her lofty voice echoing off the thick stone walls.

"That one was smuggling something," the black-haired girl tattled.

"Is that so?" the headmistress purred. "Give it here."

Sparrow watched in agonizing horror as the stone was turned over to Headmistress Greeley who rolled it around in her boney fingers. The stone was only the size of marble, but in Greeley's sharp, gloved hands it looked even more delicate.

"Brilliant, you caught a Jane smuggling a giant speck of dirt," Greeley droned with disgust.

"No, it was in her pocket. She was hiding it from us and— "

"And nothing!" Greeley bellowed, frightening the girls into silence once more. "It was probably left in her uniform from the abysmal job you do laundering them. Not another word of this nonsense or you'll be sent to the Locker where you can think about how to better perform your jobs in silence if I ever let you out at all." Greeley cast an icy glare at each of them before tossing the stone carelessly aside and leaving the dingy laundry room.

Sparrow's heart dropped. It seemed to happen in slow motion as she watched her precious floating stone roll toward the large black drain hole in the center of the floor. Once Greeley was gone, Sparrow scrambled after the stone but she was too late. It disappeared into the large black hole, which now felt as her heart did—full of darkness and despair.

9

The next morning, the strangest thing happened. A shadow loomed over Sparrow as she curled against herself trying to sleep under the drafty window in her room. The large shadow blocked the little bit of sunlight that was washing over her, stealing away her warmth. She shivered and slit her eyes open to see what was causing her discomfort. To her disbelief, Journey stood before her.

Sparrow jumped to her feet and threw her arms around him. She relished in his familiar warmth as he wrapped his arms tightly around her. "Journey, oh thank the gods! Are you all right?"

He nodded.

"Where have you been?"

"Locker."

"How did you get out?"

Journey smiled crookedly and pulled something from his pocket. Sparrow couldn't believe her eyes as he placed the tiny white stone in her hand.

"How?" she gasped breathlessly.

He smirked. "Hope floats."

Sparrow put her hands on her hips. "Journey, use your words. I'm going to need a better explanation than that."

Journey smiled and sat down in his usual spot under the window. The sight made Sparrow weak in the knees. She'd prayed and hoped and wished she'd see Journey back in their spot under the window every single night after he'd been sent to the Locker. She knelt down next to him and he folded her under his arm.

"You were right," he said. "The stone is magic. It found me in the Locker. I was sitting alone in the dark when I felt something hit my leg. I swatted at it, but something was familiar about it. I picked it up and instantly knew it was your stone and you were sending me hope. You fill me with hope, Sparrow. Enough hope to wish for a miracle and I got it."

"What do you mean?" Sparrow asked.

"I wished for a way out of the Locker and suddenly the door opened."

"How?"

"It was the stone."

"I don't understand."

"A man came down into the Locker with Greeley and some Grifts. They carried lanterns and looked around. When the man saw me he asked Greeley what I'd done. She told him and he told her to let me go."

"What? No one tells Greeley what to do. Who was this man?"

"I don't know. He never told me his name, but he had long dark hair and wore a ring with the letters MV on it."

"And Greeley just agreed to let you go?" Sparrow asked.

"No. They argued a bit. From what I could tell, the man didn't want anyone in the Locker. Greeley tried to explain that I was a problem, constantly fighting back and refusing to leave your side. That's when he called for me to come over so he could get a better look at me."

Sparrow listened intently while Journey recounted the events that took place in the Locker.

"Come here boy. Let me have a look at you," the dark-haired man called.

Journey did as he was told.

"Well, aren't you a fine specimen?" he said clicking his tongue. "This boy is too valuable to be locked away down here to rot. A big lad like him should be in the field or the forest."

"We tried to get him to mine the rubble piles, but he kept refusing unless we brought his sister out with him."

"Then shackle his sister to him. If he'll be more productive with her by his side, what do I care? We need more muscle mining those stones."

"I will not show weakness by negotiating with these filthy orphans," Greeley said sounding appalled.

"True weakness is not realizing how to exploit them to their full potential," the man replied. "This boy has given you a weapon to use against him. Watch and learn."

The dark-haired man approached Journey. He beckoned for the Grifts to unlock the cell so he could stroll in.

"It's been brought to my attention you have a sister?"

Journey nodded.

"And you want her to come work with you in the fields?"

Journey nodded again.

"If I allow this will you promise to work twice as hard as you've ever worked before?"

He nodded again.

"And you won't cause any more trouble for Headmistress Greeley?"

Another nod.

"That means you will follow all the rules from now on."

"I just want to stay with her," Journey said.

"Fine. Your wish is granted. But hear me, boy. If you do step out of line even once—I'll personally come back and kill her."

Sparrow's eyes were wide with happy tears. She couldn't believe everything Journey had been through in the Locker, but she was so relieved her stone had brought him back to her. "Journey, this proves the stone is magic. Do you believe in it now?"

"I don't know if your floating stone is magic or not, but I do believe that we are meant to be together for some reason." Journey took Sparrow's hands in his. "Sparrow I believe in us and that's all the magic I need."

Sparrow beamed. "I suppose that good enough for now."

But Sparrow was already hatching ideas for her next wish in her mind. She was surer than ever that the floating stone had magic powers. Maybe if she filled it with enough hope it would help her and Journey find a way out of the Troian Center.

10

After that night everything went back to normal. Well as normal as life enslaved at an orphanage could be. Things actually even began to improve. It seemed Journey spoke the truth. Sparrow was assigned to Flood work with him. Each day they reported to the rubble piles and sorted through debris together. Journey mined like a fiend. His basket was always twice as full as Sparrow's. He didn't want to make her look bad so he always made sure to help her fill hers up before the Grifts came to collect so she wouldn't get in any trouble.

The Janes and Johns who had tormented Sparrow while Journey was away suddenly had no interest in her now that he had returned. Some of them even shared kind words wanting to befriend her, grateful that she hadn't told Journey of their mistreatment. Sparrow ignored their false pleasantries but she did make sure to introduce Journey to the boy who'd helped her while he was in the Locker. They found him sitting in the dining hall enjoying a meal of cold fish stew.

Sparrow nervously cleared her throat. "John 18, this is John 22."

“Thanks for looking out for my friend, mate,” Journey said as he shook the green-eyed boy’s hand.

“No problem,” the boy replied. “I’m sure you’ll return the favor some day.”

Journey nodded. “Anytime. I’ve got your back, mate.”

John 18 gave a mischievous wink and sauntered away, whistling a happy tune.

WITH JOURNEY back from the Locker and Sparrow at his side again, time marched on. Days of sorting rubble and working their fingers to the bone bled together. But Sparrow was content. She had Journey and her floating stone back and life was good again. But as with all good things, they must come to an end at some point.

The air turned cool and the biting wind that chased them from the fields every afternoon told Sparrow it would soon be time for the New Year Gala. With the incredible way her floating stone seemed to be working, she made up her mind that she would ask for one more wish—for this to be the year that she and Journey would get adopted.

The night finally came for the orphans to make their annual trip to the glittering seaside city of Lux. It was the only beautiful thing to survive the Flood. All the wealthy citizens on the island resided there. Once a year the orphans were permitted to enter the city. During the New Year Gala, they would provide the entertainment—singing songs of new life and hope, while the citizens celebrated jubilantly. At the end of their performance, the orphans would all wait breathlessly to see if any of the citizens would decide to adopt them.

Each year as the paper lanterns took to the sky, Sparrow felt her hopes of adoption floating further and further away. But something felt different about this year. With the magic of her floating stone, she knew that this was the year she and Journey would finally find a home.

11

As the applause burst forth from the packed square, Sparrow could barely contain her excitement. She was on pins and needles waiting for the soloist to get off the stage. It was finally time for the citizens to choose who they would adopt. Sparrow ran to Journey's side and took his hand as she fished the white pebble from her pocket.

"Hold my hands," she said.

Journey did as he was directed.

Sparrow closed her eyes and let the hope that filled her heart radiate through her as she silently made her wish.

Please, please, please. Let this be the year that we find a home. I just want a family that loves me. And I want Journey to come with me. Please don't let us be alone anymore. Please bring us home.

When Sparrow opened her eyes, she smiled brightly up at Journey. "It's going to work," she whispered. "A family is going to pick us tonight. I just know it."

Journey stoically nodded as they followed the group of orphans, being slowly ushered toward the stage.

EPILOGUE

The walk home was excruciating for Sparrow. She'd been so sure that someone would adopt her and Journey. And for a moment she thought the floating stone had worked and her wish had come true. But it was someone else's wish that the gods granted. A girl standing to Sparrow's right had been adopted, plucked from refuse—brought to the life of luxury and light.

A deep feeling of emptiness washed over Sparrow. It was strange to feel heavy and hollow all at once, but she did. When the group stopped next to a pond for a rest halfway back to the Troian Center, Sparrow could no long mask her tears. They slide from her eyes like marbles on glass.

Journey pulled her to him, letting Sparrow bury her face in his chest.

"I'm so stupid," she whispered.

"Why?" he asked.

"Because I wished that the floating stone would bring us a family tonight. And I let myself get so hopeful ... " She trailed off stifling a sob. "You were right. There isn't any magic in this stone. It's just a stupid rock."

Journey gently pulled at Sparrow's chin so she would look up at him. His amber eyes grew serious as he gazed into hers. "Sparrow, it's not stupid if it gives you hope."

"But you don't even believe in it," she whimpered.

"But I believe in you, remember. You're my family, Sparrow. We don't need anyone else."

Sparrow felt her heart swell as she stared into Journey's warm amber eyes. They reminded her of her mother's eyes and it broke her heart every time that thought crossed her mind. But Journey was right. Maybe her mother hadn't sent her the stone or Journey. Maybe finding the floating stone had merely been a coincidence that offered Sparrow a false hope she had needed to survive. Perhaps it was time for her to stop living on hope alone.

In order to escape the crippling disappointment that plagued her when her wishes didn't come true, Sparrow knew she would have to let go of some things. She closed her eyes and let the tears spill out as she tried to let go of the hope of ever seeing her mother again and the idea that a nice family would adopt her and Journey someday. Sparrow was beginning to realize some things could never be and it was time to grow up.

But as Journey wiped her tears away she realized that he was right. They had each other and he believed in her. Maybe that was the only kind of hope she needed. The real kind.

"You're right," she said taking a deep breath. Sparrow's heart tore as she let go of her belief in magic and threw the useless stone into the nearby pond. And this time it sank.

The Paths We Cannot See

A SHORT STORY

C.J. Benjamin

FOREWORD

The Paths We Cannot See

Life is a journey of intersecting paths,
Beginning when a single uncertain step, is stepped.
You may not know what path you are on,
but you are on it nonetheless.

Your path may lead you where you shan't expect.
To paths we cannot see.
At times your paths will cross with others,
Never knowing how long with you they shall be.

Some paths converge only for a moment,
Never to meet again.
While others crisscross repeatedly,
Every now and then.

Many paths run along together,
Leaving within us, a deep and momentous groove.
These paths form friendships you will carry,

No matter where your paths shall move.

Some paths are rare and precious,
Presented as a gift.
Some paths shall try to tempt us,
Meant to send you adrift.

Some paths will require you to forge them,
While others will be well traveled.
Some are meant to be trekked alone,
And some to be unraveled.

If love should shine upon you,
And invite another to your path.
Count your many blessings,
For your soul another soul now hath.

Revel in love's splendid company,
For you no longer walk alone.
Join hands and hearts together,
And blaze a new path, all your own.

Though many paths exist for us,
And no map lies in wait,
The important thing to remember is,
No two paths are the same.

Dear traveler heed my warning,
No matter where you stray.
It matters not what path you choose,
But that you keep your heart open along the way.

PROLOGUE

The Unforgiving Sea

There once lived a man whose sorrow was vast,
He could do nothing but dwell on his past.

He longed for the faces and places he'd lost,
His life passed him by, never taking note of the paths
he now crossed.

Soon he found himself withered and old,
In no time it would be for he, whom the bell tolled.

Dismayed at how his life had been wasted,
He vowed to spend his last days unhasted.

So many were the paths he could have chose,
If he hadn't been blinded by his sorrowful heart's
woes.

He took the path now before him,
Searching for someone whose future was grim.

Upon finding a sullen young boy,
The old man shared his wisdom with joy.

"Pick your head up boy, and open your eyes,
There are many more options for you than you realize."

"Take it from me, for my wasted life I abhor.
Too busy chasing memories to even see I had a chance to make more."

"But Sir, can't you see my heart has been broken?
I can take no comfort in the words you have spoken."

But the man stood his ground knowing he still had more to give.
Clearing his throat he announced,
"It is no good to dwell on the past and forget how to live."

1

Ivy's laughter filled the air as Nova chased after her on the beach. Her wavy blonde hair bounced behind her, riding the currents of the salt air. She shrieked with delight every time he reached for her and missed. Of course he could have caught his baby sister without much trouble, but letting her think she could beat him was half the fun.

Nothing rivaled Ivy's smile. She had a way of wrapping Nova around her little finger. From the moment Ivy was born he knew he'd do anything for his little sister. He'd never felt the need to protect something so fiercely. With her sparkling sea-green eyes and a smile that lit up Nova's world, he had trouble telling the tenacious toddler 'no', which resulted in many trips to the beach—Ivy's favorite place in the world.

Nova worried about the way his little sister longed for the water. It was as if the water spoke to Ivy, luring her toward its dangerous depths. Her voice pulled Nova from his disturbing thoughts. "Catch me, Nova! Catch me!" she squealed as she raced into the water.

"No! Ivy, you can't swim."

She giggled and waded out further, taunting him. "Come get me, Nova!"

Nova's heart plummeted as he watched a ravenous wave building behind Ivy. He was on his feet in an instant. Nova sprinted forward but he couldn't move fast enough. No matter how far he ran the beach extended further. "Ivy, look out!"

Nova screamed as he watched the wave crash over his sister. He plunged into the dark, frigid water. It took his breath away. The shore dipped away quickly and he had to fight against a strong current to get to Ivy. He grabbed for her hand but missed as a hungry swell pulled her under. White foam frothed savagely, blocking Nova's view. Ivy's frantic voice carried across the water. "Nova! Don't leave me!"

Something slammed into Nova's chest, hard. "Ivy!" he screamed.

The pain came again, harder this time. But Nova was determined to get to his sister. "Ivy!"

This time the blow to his chest was so hard he was gasping for air. He felt something smothering his face and everything went dark.

A VOICE HISSED in Nova's ear. "Wake up, 18! And stop screaming or you're going to get us all sent to the Locker!"

Nova heard movement around him, but he couldn't see anything.

"I think you're suffocating him," a voice warned and suddenly there was light.

Nova struggled to get his bearings and when he did, the painful ache in his chest only grew worse. *It was just a dream. It was always just a dream.* Ivy was dead. Nova would never see his sister again—unless it was in his nightmares.

Nova sat up in his bed, and two boys stared back at him angrily; one was holding a pillow.

"Were you trying to smother me?" Nova accused, noting the suspicious grasp the boy had on the pillow.

"If it would keep us outta trouble," the boy shot back smugly. "I'm not going to the Locker for you, 18. I don't care how tough everyone says you are."

"Sorry," Nova mumbled getting up from the bed. He ran his hand through his golden curls. They were drenched with sweat. "I didn't know I was talking in my sleep."

"You weren't just talking, you were screaming."

"You didn't seem so invincible then," the other boy snickered.

"I said I'm sorry," Nova growled as he walked to his wardrobe to dress.

"Not good enough," the boy said dropping the pillow to shove Nova.

Nova anticipated the boy's next move and easily dodged it, quickly pinning his arm painfully behind his back. "Don't push me," Nova snarled. "Not today."

By now most of the orphans in the room had woken, and Nova had an audience. Something he didn't want. He shoved the boy away and tried to ignore their stares as he quickly dressed.

In his years at the Troian Center Nova had gained quite the reputation as a fighter. He'd spent his early years angry that the Flood had stolen his family, and he lashed out at anyone who gave him an excuse. By the time he'd reached his teens he had built an undefeated record on scarred knuckles, lean muscles and a cocky attitude. He'd never lost a fight and with a reputation like that, he had to watch his back. It seemed someone was always waiting in the wings to prove themselves—hoping to be the one to strip Nova of that title.

Of course, they didn't stand a chance. *But they didn't know that.* The rest of the orphans at the Troian Center had no idea of Nova's mind reading abilities—which made getting a jump on him nearly impossible. The only time he was ever truly vulnerable was when he was asleep, stuck in his terrifying nightmares or lonely dreams.

Nova opened and closed his fists. It would be too easy. He could defeat the two dimwitted boys who still leered at him with his eyes closed. But if the whole room turned on him it might be a challenge. Definitely one that would earn him a trip to the Locker, and that was somewhere he didn't want to be. Not today.

Nova took a deep breath and pushed passed the boys. "Go back to bed before you hurt yourself."

He grabbed his bag and stalked out of the room. It was dawn, almost time to start the day and he needed some air to get his head right. He slipped into the dark hallway, moving silently with the shadows, toward the only place that ever gave him any peace—the courtyard.

Years ago Nova had discovered a hole in the courtyard wall hidden by a giant banana palm. It's where he went when he needed to be alone or think. Today was definitely one of those days. It'd snuck up on him, but it was there nonetheless. It explained the nightmares. He had the same one every year around this time—his sister Ivy's birthday. Or it would have been, had the Flood not stolen her.

When the Flood hit, Nova's world had been turned upside down. His entire family had been lost in the legendary storm that nearly destroyed Hullabee Island. Nova remembered every detail of that fateful day—running through the smoke filled forest with his family, dodging the lava and raging waters. When they found themselves trapped in the forest with smoke too thick to see through, Nova's father lifted him into a tree and commanded him to climb as high as he could. "Don't look back, and don't let go, son." Nova argued that he didn't want to leave them, but his father was insistent. He could still hear his mother's last words to him. "We'll never leave you, son. Have faith," she said as she clutched Ivy. A wet gray cloth covered his sister's head to help her breathe through the smoke, but her sea-green eyes shone brightly as she put her hand to her lips sending him a final kiss.

Nova obeyed his father's orders and climbed the tree. He clung to it for dear life and somehow survived the Flood. But the rest of his family hadn't been so lucky. He spent days frantically searching for them in the charred forest, but they were gone. Swept out to sea with all the other poor souls that the gods hadn't thought to spare.

Nova finally reached his hiding spot in the courtyard. He slipped behind the palm and reached for the hole in the coquina wall. He was tall enough to see through it easily now. The opening gave him the perfect view of the beach beyond. He closed his eyes and drank in the salty sea air in long desperate gulps, letting its warm currents lick away the tears that escaped his eyes. He swiped at them angrily as he stared at the sea. It brought him comfort and heartache simultaneously. He wondered if the sea would ever stop reminding him of Ivy. Sometimes he swore he could still hear her laughter in the calls of the shorebirds or her voice in the crash of the waves. Nova gazed out at the sea—deep blues and greens with gold painted across the top where the sun kissed the water. Winking stars—that's what Ivy had said the sunlight on the water looked like.

On days like today the tranquil blue waters made Nova feel murderous. *How could something so calm and beautiful be so deadly?* It had stolen everything he'd ever loved and broken his heart to bits, leaving an infinite emptiness in his chest that could never be put back together. He glared at the endless expense of blue. The immensity of it made him feel so helpless. Each time the lapping waves retreated from the shore he felt as if they were stealing his family from him once more. He punched his fist into the wall and closed his eyes against the pain. In the end he knew he was powerless against the unforgiving sea.

2

Thinking about his family was always painful for Nova. But Ivy's birthday was the worst day for him. He hated the thought of letting another year go by where no one celebrated Ivy's birthday. He'd always had a hard time with the idea that just because someone was gone you had to go on without them. It was forbidden to speak of those lost in the Flood for fear of angering the gods. That's why all the orphans at the Trioan Center had been striped of their names and tattooed with numbers instead. The Flood was a cleansing, and those who survived were given a second chance to start over, and that apparently meant with a new name and no mention of the past.

But not today, Nova thought. Today would be different. He didn't know how, but he was determined to find a way to honor his sister's birthday this year.

Nova's temper was tightly coiled by the time he lined up for Flood work. He'd made it through breakfast and lessons but was haunted by the fact that soon the sun would be setting, and he hadn't thought of a way to celebrate Ivy's birthday yet. He hadn't had a chance. The strenuous schedule at the Troian Center didn't really leave time for frivolous endeavors.

At least Nova had graduated to forest duty last year. That meant each day, during Flood work, he and all the other able bodied boys in his year or older would be sent out to the rainforest to mine Flood debris. They would load up horse drawn carts with their day's work and lead them back to the rubble piles for the younger orphans to sort. It was hard, physical labor—splitting rocks with a pickaxe and sweating in the humid afternoon sun of the rainforest. Nova always came back exhausted and drenched in sweat, but he actually looked forward to it. There was no better way to expend his pent up frustration of being imprisoned at the orphanage. Well, no better way that didn't result in a trip to the Locker.

Nova's quick temper and smart mouth had made him a fixture in the Locker. But it was another place he didn't mind. He'd learned to enjoy his time there. It at least offered solitude. And he had his own little tricks for making himself more comfortable in the dark dungeon under the Troian Center —*light!*

A few years back, Nova had discovered some very interesting qualities about himself. He knew as soon as he arrived at the Troian Center that he wasn't like everyone else. He could hear what people were thinking, and project his thoughts into their minds—a handy tool for getting what he wanted or for amusement when he was bored. But his favorite trick was discovered when he was stuck in the Locker. In a desperate moment he somehow managed to conjure a flame at will. He'd perfected the art during his time spent in the Locker for pranks or fighting. He could now wield a single flame in the palm of his hand. With the aid of his flame, he'd found all kinds of ways to distract himself in the Locker, but he was most interested in the writing on the walls.

At first he'd been excited, thinking he'd found some sort of ancient secret that would lead him out of the Locker and the Troian Center for good. With thoughts of freedom fueling him, Nova read feverishly. He even found himself doing all sorts of devious things just for more chances to get sent to the Locker so he could continue reading. But after years of studying the legends and trying to decipher them, Nova began to feel foolish to think that they would lead anywhere. They certainly wouldn't give him the happy ending he'd been wishing for since he came to the awful orphanage—one where he'd sail far away from Hullabee Island in search of his family.

After too many disappointing dead ends, Nova would have given up on the legends had he not met Ren. Ren was one of the locals that helped mine debris in the forest and one of the only adults Nova liked. Ren always had a smile on his face. He spoke softly and was full of colorful stories of brighter times before the Flood had ravaged Hullabee Island. It also helped that sometimes he'd get so lost in his own storytelling that he wouldn't notice when Nova would sneak away to stare at the sea and reflect on all he'd lost.

After a while Nova began to trust Ren. They spoke about their families and things they enjoyed before the Flood. Ren had lost his home and family too and now had to work mining debris in order to pay room and board at a little village near the Troian Center. They bonded over their losses and eventually, Nova trusted Ren enough to tell him about what he'd found in the Locker.

Nova had never seen an adult so excited. He would have thought he told Ren he could go live in the Tower of Lux or something. Ren was a fanatic about all the myths and legends of the island and couldn't believe Nova had found so many of them etched into the walls under the Troian Center. He made Nova describe everything he read, and they discussed it at length. Ren was of the belief that the Legend of Lux was real—a prophecy that foretold of the Eva, who would someday come to Hullabee Island to restore peace and glory, bringing light to all that was bathed in darkness after the Flood. Nova was still unsure what he believed.

3

On the afternoon of what would have been Ivy's birthday, Nova worked out his frustrations silently alongside Ren, who was merrily singing with the other workers. Nova never joined in. It's not that he didn't like music. In fact he used to love it. His father had taught him how to play the gourd guitar, and his family used to sit around their fireplace at night and sing. He still remembered how Ivy would bounce on his lap while they sang. Music had been a source of joy in Nova's life. But the Flood had stolen that too. Like everything else, music was just a painful memory now.

Nova was doing a good job tuning out the songs until his least favorite ballad was called up, filling the forest with its haunting melody.

'COME THEE, *come thee,*
all will come, yet none will see.
Lost are we, are we,
the forgotten children you refuse to see.

Hollow are we, are we,
for our parents and hearts were returned to the sea.
The sea, the sea. The unforgiving sea.'

"I REALLY COULD DO without this song," Nova grumbled.

"Singing passes the time," Ren said with his usual optimism. "You should try it some time. Frees the soul. Besides, what's wrong with this song?"

"Can't a person just hate a particular song?" Nova huffed.

Ren let out a soft chuckle. "I would've thought this would be a favorite of yours, what with the way you're always gazing at the ocean."

"Well, it's not," Nova muttered swinging his axe to split a massive fossilized tree stump. "It's depressing."

"Says the boy who stares at the world like he wants to set it on fire."

"Maybe I do," Nova replied hotly.

"Listen, son. Life's not always fair, but all we can do is make the best of it."

Nova grunted as he swung his axe again. "Why bother? There's nothing left for me on this gods forsaken island. The Flood stole my whole family. What do I possibly have to live for?"

Ren's withered lips quirked into a soft smile. "I know your pain, son. The Flood took my family too. But it was the gods that caused the Flood. And it was the gods that spared you. No use hating them. No use hating anything really. It won't bring back what we've lost. I've told you that before. That temper of yours is no good. All we can do now is hope."

"Hope for what? You just said nothing would bring my family back and that's all I want."

"There's always hope, son. You gotta hold onto hope that

things will get better, hope that you'll find your purpose, hope for the Eva."

Nova snorted.

"Don't scoff at things you know nothing about," Ren warned.

"I know all about the Eva, the bringer of light, the savior of this gods forsaken island. It's all you ever talk about. But I've been at the Troian Center for years, Ren, and I'm running out of hope. I need a little more to go on than myths and legends."

"What's gotten into you today?"

"Nothing."

"Don't tell me nothing. We've been hauling stone outta this forest together for nearly a year. I can tell something's wrong. What's eatin' ya?"

Nova dropped his head and stared at his worn shoes. "Today's Ivy's birthday."

"Why didn't you say so?" Ren asked putting a comforting arm across Nova's tan shoulders. "I'm sorry, son."

For a moment they both stared silently at the sea. Then Ren spoke. "I've been saving something for a special occasion, and this seems to be it." He pulled a small white stone no bigger than his thumbnail from his pocket. He kissed it and grabbed Nova's hand, pressing the stone into his palm.

"This is your lucky stone," Nova said.

"And now it's yours."

"Ren, I can't take this."

"You can, and you will. I'm an old man. I've filled that stone with a lifetime of hope. I have no one left to give it to. But maybe you do."

Nova stared at the white stone. It felt so light in his hand, so ordinary. He knew Ren believed it was a mythical Floating Stone—a magic stone that could carry messages of hope from land to sea and back. Nova knew the story well. It was famous on Hullabee Island, as were many mariner tales. But Nova didn't believe it was true. He wasn't sure if he believed in anything anymore.

Ren spoke kindly. "You need hope most when you feel it is lost. Never give up hope, son. Hope will always float."

Nova's eyes stung, and he bit back against the tightness in his throat, looking down at the ground again. He used to hope for many things—to have a family again, to be loved, to have a real home, a purpose. More than anything he hoped to leave Hullabee Island and his horrible memories behind and start a new life somewhere else. Anywhere else. He even hoped he could have found a way to honor Ivy on her birthday. But he knew hoping for all of those things was useless. They were just dreams. Nova had learned to push his hopes away. They made him weak. And the weak were preyed upon at the Troian Center.

"Ren, I really appreciate it. But I don't want to waste this," Nova said trying to hand the stone back. "I don't have anything to hope for."

"Nonsense. Today's your Ivy's birthday. Why don't you send her a birthday wish?"

"How?"

"March down to that beach, and tell her all your hopes and dreams. Tell her what's in your heart. That you love her and miss her and you're thinking of her on her birthday."

"She can't hear me, Ren. She's dead." Nova choked on his own harsh words.

"Well of course she won't hear you if you won't do it."

Nova glared at Ren.

"Quit your sulkin' and get down to that beach and send your wish into the sea. If your sister's somewhere out there, she'll hear you."

"You don't know that she will."

"And you don't know that she won't," he said with a twinkle

in his gray eyes. His smile pushed the deep wrinkles on his face together like ripples of water. "Go on. I'll cover for you."

Nova sighed and headed down the steep incline to the beach. Ren was as stubborn as a mule, and Nova knew there was no use arguing.

4

Nova kicked off his shoes and dug his toes into the cool, wet sand. A memory flashed through his mind —Ivy, burying him in the sand and giggling wildly when he would wiggle his way out. Nova stared out at the sea, letting it conjure up bittersweet memories—playing with Ivy on the beach, laughing with his family in the waves, building sandcastles, collecting seashells. They should have had a lifetime to do those things together. But Nova's memories were all he had left of his family now. An inkling of what should have been if the Flood hadn't come and stolen everyone he loved.

He stared at the ocean as pain coursed through him. The constant whisper of the sea awoke an ache in his heart that made him hope that his family might still be out there—that they might have somehow survived the Flood. Perhaps the sea carried them away somewhere safe. *It had to be possible or why would he still feel their loss so strongly?*

The sighs from the waves called to Nova, whispering his name. He swiped at the tears that swelled in his eyes. Nova longed to hear someone say his name again. It's been so long since he'd heard it. No one at the Troian Center knew his real name. Not even Ren. Nova wondered if he would ever trust anyone enough to share it. He yearned for someone to speak his name like his family had—full of love, pride, joy. He missed the way it sounded when his mother whispered it, or Ivy shrieked it, or his father called it across the fields.

Nova took a step closer to the water, straining to hear the words on the crashing waves. He could see why Ivy loved the sea so much. Its pull was magnetizing. This wasn't the first time Nova found himself wondering if perhaps he could join his family in its deep waters. Nova shook himself from his trance, knowing no answers lay at the bottom of the sea. And Ren was right; Nova had been saved for a purpose. He didn't know what it was yet, but he was determined to find out. He squeezed the stone in his palm—with any luck, the stone would show him his path.

Nova let his last thread of hope fill his chest. He hadn't let himself unlock his heart in so long. Living at the Troian Center had made him grow up fast and hide his emotions. Emotions were what got you hurt. He'd been taught the things he loved would be taken away, and he didn't want to let himself be vulnerable in that way anymore.

One last time, Nova thought. *I'll play along and beg to all the gods one last time and then I'll lock it all away for good.*

Nova looked up and down the beach to make sure he was alone. It was deserted and the crashing waves drowned out the noise of the workers far above him. He clutched the white stone to his chest and took a deep breath, drinking in the warm salt air.

"Ivy, I just want you to know how much I love you. And that I think of you every day. Especially today. I'm so sorry I failed you. It should have been you that lived. It was my job to protect you, and I failed." He choked back his tears. "Gods, I'm begging you, if my family is out there send me a sign. Send me some way to find them. Because if I knew there was a way . . . if I could have love again . . . have my family, my home . . . nothing would stop me from making that happen."

With that Nova brought the stone to his lips and whispered. "Happy birthday, Ivy. I wish I could find my way back to you." He kissed the pale white stone and heaved it into the sea.

5

Nova closed his eyes as he waited—hoping and praying he hadn't been taken for a fool. *The gods are probably laughing at me,* he thought as he took deep breaths and counted to twenty before opening his eyes.

When he opened them everything looked the same. The setting sun sprayed the sea with glittering flecks of gold and bronze. The shore birds glided over the waves, and the frothing sea-green water lapped at his feet. Nova shook his head. "I'm a fool," he muttered as he turned to gather his shoes. But a rouge wave crashed, and the surf raced passed him, soaking him to the knees.

"Great!" he yelled as he chased his sopping shoes and pulled them from the receding surf. "Just perfect!"

As the water raced back to the sea, shells and seaweed tumbled passed Nova. A hunk of silver rolled toward him, stopping with an unceremonious thud when it hit his foot. Nova stared at the strange looking object. It was metal, but looked like it had been buried in the ocean for quite a while from the barnacles that had latched to it. He reached down to pick it up, and a tiny fiddler crab leapt from one of the shells that had tried to claim the metal as its home.

Nova pried off the other crustaceans and buffed the round metal lump on his shirttails. It gleamed the fading sunlight back at him. He could make out a faint pattern etched into the top. Nova huffed his breath onto the metal and rubbed it with his thumb to bring the pattern out. Suddenly it began to vibrate and the lid sprang open revealing a whirling of intricate gears.

Nova released an astonished breath. It was a compass, but unlike one he'd ever seen before. Hope sang through his veins as he tried to tamp his excitement. *Could this be the sign he'd asked for?* It had to be. The floating stone had worked!

Nova jammed his feet into his soggy shoes and sprinted from the beach. He had to find Ren and show him what he'd found.

6

"Well I'll be!" Ren exclaimed, his gray eyes wide and sparkling. "Do you have any idea what this is, son?"

"A strange compass?"

"This is Death's arrow."

Nova exhaled, the excitement leaving his body. "That doesn't sound good."

"It all depends whose hand it's in," Ren replied. "The legend says that this was the tool Death used to find those in the great book and reap their souls when their time in this realm was up. But a jealous fairy bewitched it so it would only show a heart's true desire. Being without a heart, Death was furious he could not make his compass work. Death hated being cheated so he took his compass to the best Timekeepers in the land but none could break the fairy's curse. It's believed that this compass has been passed around through the ages, finding those who need it. It's part of many legends and known under different names."

"Are these good legends or bad?" Nova asked warily.

"That depended on who possessed the compass. If it was

someone of a pure heart, it brought good tidings—love, health, happiness. If it was wielded by someone without a pure heart, it fetched greed, death, malice." Ren placed the heavy compass into Nova's hand. "Great responsibility had been bestowed upon you, son. Use it wisely."

"You really think this is a magic compass?" Nova asked skeptically.

Ren nodded.

"Why did it choose me?"

"You called it."

"No I didn't. I wished for hope."

Ren chuckled softly. "Hope comes to us in many ways, and often when we need it most. You've been searching for a purpose, this will help you find it."

"But I don't know what I'm supposed to look for."

"It's in here," Ren said poking a rough finger into Nova's chest. "Follow your heart, son."

7

For two weeks straight Nova followed the strange compass without any results.

"I think it's broken. Maybe it was in the bottom of the sea for too long or something."

"Why do you say that?" Ren asked.

"All it's done it get me sent to the Locker, pointed at the same legend over and over and made me follow around a scrawny orphan girl."

Ren scratched his coarse gray beard for a moment. "What legend?"

"The same one as yesterday. The one about the Eva; the Legend of Lux."

"And it's the same girl?"

"Always. The tiny blonde one, #65."

"So it's a pattern?"

"Yes. That's what I'm trying to tell you. Legend—girl. Legend—girl."

Ren fought to hide a grin. His wild facial hair helped disguise it, but his eyes gave him away. Their rare gray color always gleamed when he smiled.

"Well . . ." Nova said impatiently. "I know you have a theory. You always have a theory."

"It seems you've already figured it out."

"What are you talking about? All I've figured out is that every day this stupid lump of metal drags me to the same stupid legend and the same girl."

"So . . ."

"So what? You think the legend is about the girl?"

"I always knew you were a smart boy."

"Okay, first of all, there's no way that's true. 65 is an orphan. She has the same terrible fate as me. Plus she's a pipsqueak, always walking around on her tippy toes, getting into trouble. She's in the Locker almost as much as I am. There's no way she's the Eva that's supposed to save us all. And besides, even if I believed in the legend, it only proves that this thing is broken."

"How so?"

"It's not what I asked for. Finding the Eva isn't my heart's true desire."

"What is?"

Nova clammed up.

"I know this is a personal question, son, but what did you wish for when you cast the floating stone into the sea?"

Nova felt his cheeks flush. It wasn't easy for him to trust others. But this was Ren. His powers told him what the man was thinking and he could tell Ren was only trying to help. Nova looked at the fossilized stump his axe rested on, unable to meet Ren's eyes as he spoke. "Home, family . . . love."

"Ah, wise man."

Nova only stared at Ren with confusion.

Ren sighed and put his hand comfortingly on Nova's shoulder. "Son, sometimes the universe gives us what we ask for, but not it the way we think. We need to be open to receive the gifts the gods bring us. This compass was a gift. It's led you to something; to a girl. Maybe she seeks the same things you do—home, family, love. Maybe you'll find it together. Maybe you'll be it for each other. Maybe you'll help her bring it to this whole island. But you'll never know unless you let yourself be open to the possibilities."

Nova let Ren's words sink it. They felt familiar. Like Nova's own heart had been trying to trace the same thoughts, but his practical mind fought him.

"You've been presented with purpose, son. You've been given a path. Follow it, as only you can."

Nova nodded, feeling a light grow inside him. "You're right, Ren. Thank you."

He flipped the compass closed with purpose. Nova had made up his mind. He was going to follow this path and see where it could take him. He'd start by talking to 65. *After all, how much trouble could talking to the girl be?*

8

With Ren's words echoing in Nova's mind, he mustered up his courage and approached the petite girl with the flaxen curls and unsettling blue eyes—Jane 65. He'd been watching her for weeks, observing her habits, eavesdropping on her thoughts. He knew it was cheating. The poor girl had no idea that he could read her mind, but the more Nova learned about her the more endearing she became to him.

She was small but scrappy. She didn't let her size stop her. She stuck up for herself and her friend—a mousy boy with a mop of brown hair. She had a bit of a smart mouth and a sarcastic sense of humor. Nova loved watching her laugh. He couldn't help but grin when her freckles danced on her smiling cheeks, or when her stunning blue eyes sparkled each time she was happy. But for all her bravado, she was just as full of self-doubt and sadness as Nova was. Maybe even more. It made him want to hug her and tell her she wasn't alone.

As Nova drew closer to the rubble pile, he noticed 65 was talking to something. He paused to listen. When he realized she was speaking to the stone she was polishing his nerves evaporated. Ivy used to do the same thing. She'd talk to all the shells and sea glass she collected from the beach. Nova grinned and found himself wanting to tell 65, but he had to stop himself. He didn't want to freak her out.

He took a deep breath and murmured his mother's words to himself for courage. "Have faith."

With a few brisk strides he was alongside 65 at the rubble pile. "So, is that your best friend or what?"

She jumped and threw the stone. Nova instantly regretted startling her. He probably shouldn't have led with that, but something about the girl disarmed him. He didn't know exactly what to say to her, yet he felt oddly comfortable around her.

"Why did you do that?" she screamed. "Now I have to find it and start all over."

"Jeez, sorry kid, I wasn't trying to scare you. I've just never heard anyone talk to a rock before," he lied.

"It's not a rock!" she huffed. "It's a ruby! And don't call me kid!"

"Okay, okay, I'll help you find it if you stop shouting about it. You're gonna get us sent to the Locker."

She glared at Nova but the mention of the Locker seemed to bring her back to reality. She scanned the fields to make sure none of the Grifts had noticed her outburst. The fear in her startling blue eyes made Nova feel terrible. He had a sudden urge to protect her. He didn't want anything to make her feel that frightened.

"So what's your name, kid?" Nova whispered as he helped her search for the stone she'd dropped.

"65," she replied curtly.

He smiled and extended his hand. "I'm Nova."

9

Nova ran to the forest. He couldn't wait to tell Ren he'd spoken to 65, and he was convinced the compass had been right. They had a connection.

Nova was breathless by the time he reached the mining crew deep within the forest. A glistening sheen of sweat clung to every inch of his tan skin. He wiped his brow with the hem of his shirt.

"18! Where've you been?" boomed a loud voice behind him.

Nova spun to meet the face of an angry Grift.

"You're late for work."

Strange, Nova thought. Ren always covered for him. "Uh, sorry, Sir. I was helping Ren with one of the stubborn horses." That was the excuse they always used to get the Grifts off their backs.

"Really?" The Grift smirked cynically. "I find that hard to believe since Ren passed away last night."

The air rushed from Nova's lungs. "What?"

"Are you hard of hearing, boy? Ren's dead! I helped carry him to the pyre this morning so don't try making up any other wild tales."

9

Nova ran to the forest. He couldn't wait to tell Ren he'd spoken to 65, and he was convinced the compass had been right. They had a connection.

Nova was breathless by the time he reached the mining crew deep within the forest. A glistening sheen of sweat clung to every inch of his tan skin. He wiped his brow with the hem of his shirt.

"18! Where've you been?" boomed a loud voice behind him.

Nova spun to meet the face of an angry Grift.

"You're late for work."

Strange, Nova thought. Ren always covered for him. "Uh, sorry, Sir. I was helping Ren with one of the stubborn horses." That was the excuse they always used to get the Grifts off their backs.

"Really?" The Grift smirked cynically. "I find that hard to believe since Ren passed away last night."

The air rushed from Nova's lungs. "What?"

"Are you hard of hearing, boy? Ren's dead! I helped carry him to the pyre this morning so don't try making up any other wild tales."

Nova's racing pulse thundered in his ears drowning out the rest of the Grift's rude comments. It wasn't until a blow from the Grift knocked Nova to the ground that the world came back into focus. The Grift landed a solid whack to the side of Nova's head causing him to bite his tongue. He winced in shock as he spat blood. Usually his unique abilities allowed him to predict and avoid such abuse. He blinked up at the ruthless Grift with hatred.

"Get back to work, 18, and if I hear any lip from you or any more lies you'll end up in the Locker faster than you can spell it."

Nova's mind was reeling. Ren had been a staple in his life—his one source of friendship, kindness, happiness. Nova had shared so much with him. Ren knew more of Nova than anyone else on Hullabee Island. And Nova still had so much to tell him.

He wanted to tell him he'd met 65. And Ren had been right! In one strange conversation Nova had felt a spark—a strange and powerful connection that whispered of legends and magic deep within his bones. 65 was like Nova, he knew she was. Maybe she was even the Eva! Just one touch had convinced Nova, and all he wanted to do was share that with Ren—the only other person who would understand. Nova wanted to thank him for the floating stone that brought the compass to him. He wanted to apologize for not believing in all the magic and legends that Ren shared with him. He wanted to say so many things. Like how he believed in the legends and the compass, and that it had brought him to a girl who'd awoken his heart. She released it from its tortured cage and filled Nova with light. He'd finally found what he was searching for—purpose—someone worth fighting for.

But Ren was gone and Nova would never get to say any of those things.

Nova worked in lonely silence for the rest of his shift, letting the devastating loss of Ren wash over him. He knew Ren would be upset to see Nova sad. He'd say something like, *buck up,* or *make lemonade outta lemons.* Nova sighed. He would miss Ren and his quirky optimism, but he knew the best way to honor him would be to stay strong and not let the hope and kindness Ren had brought into his life be wasted.

When the workers began to head back toward the Troian Center, Nova took his chance to slip away from the group and sneak down to the beach. He clutched the heavy compass in his hand, letting its weight sink in.

"I guess it's time to send you back to the sea," Nova said. "I've found what I was looking for. I don't need you anymore."

The words stung as he said them. It felt as though he was saying them to Ren. And perhaps Nova didn't need Ren, but he would miss him.

Nova squared his shoulders and closed his eyes. As the sun set, he took a deep breath and imagined his friend sailing away on a peaceful sea to be reunited with those he'd loved and lost. "Farewell my friend. I will carry your faith and continue to hope."

And with that, Nova heaved the compass back into the unforgiving sea.

10

Nova walked back toward the Troian Center. When he reached the forest's edge he gazed across the fields to the rest of the Flood workers. Where the paths converged he could see the slight silhouette of 65 still working on the rubble pile. Despite the tragedy of the day, for the first time, Nova felt the hollowness in his heart shrink. He knew he was still facing an uncertain future, but when he looked at 65 he knew he wasn't facing it alone.

A SHORT STORY

C.J. Benjamin

FOREWORD

Wind and loam,
I call thee to thy bone.
Across the heavens you have blown,
Your power harnessed as my own.
Though full heart and spirit have yet grown,
Thy gift bestowed was always known.

PROLOGUE

There once was a weeping willow tree,
Born of melancholy tears and ash shed unto thee.
Beneath its lonesome boughs love grew free,
But in its somber shade loss would ever be.
To lay below its veil one can never see,
The dangers of such a life of weeping be.

1

Jovi stood under the massive weeping willow tree. *Weeping*, what a proper description for the tree that housed the remains of her family. She knelt among the roots, letting her fingers trace the names that had been etched into the bark.

Kyo Ventus

Neho Ventus

Talon Ventus

As she caressed the names of each of her beloved and lost family members, she felt as though she was carving them into her own heart, so as not to forget them on her long journey to the Tower of Lux.

It would be the furthest she'd ever traveled from her home in the rainforest. And she knew there was a possibility she might never return.

Jovi sunk her hands into the soil and let her tears pour into the dark earth. She couldn't help remembering the first time her mother brought her to the willow tree. It's what sealed her fate and simultaneously broke her mother's heart.

2

Jovi was only a child when it happened. So young she didn't clearly remember her age, only the events of that day. It was something she could never forget.

Her mother made a yearly pilgrimage to the mystical weeping willow tree that had grown deep within the Beto rainforest. The trees didn't exist on Hullabee Island, but legend said this one had sprouted from the pureness of love of the tears wept there. It was Jovi's mother, Vida, who had planted her seeds of loss. At the base of the tree, Vida buried the ashes of her husband and called to the lost soul of her son, whose body had never been recovered from the Flood.

Jovi begged year after year to come along and finally her mother allowed it. Jovi remembered everything about that day. The way the sun dappled her skin as it soaked through the morning mist. How she rode the whole way to the willow tree on her big brother, Talon's, shoulders. She always loved being so high above the ground. The way the breeze ruffled her hair and whispered its secrets to her was alluring.

When they arrived at the weeping willow, Jovi remembered thinking it was the saddest tree she'd ever seen. She crawled beneath its boughs and tried to hug her tiny arms around the vast trunk. She looked up at the names of her father and brother whom she'd never met and began to cry. Vida knelt next to her daughter, gently stroking her wild hair.

"It's not fair, Mama. I never even got to meet them."

"I know. But they are still with you. Their love touches you through the sun every day and the stars every night."

"But I still miss them."

"When you miss them, you can come here and feel their presence around you, deep in the earth."

Jovi smiled at her mother and gave her a hug. She sat by watching as her mother and brother each took a private moment to kneel before the names etched into the bark, confiding their secret messages to her father and brother. When it was Jovi's turn she didn't know what to do. She mimicked her family and put her tiny hands on the bark, tracing their names. But as she touched them she felt her heart constrict with pain and she wondered how it was possible to miss people she hadn't met. But she did. She felt their loss in her bones and she dug her hands into the soil and began to cry.

That's when everything changed.

3

Jovi hadn't even noticed at first. It was her mother's cries that alerted her of the disturbance. But when she looked up it wasn't fear that gripped her, but wonder. The boughs of the willow tree had come alive. They danced around her, trembling with iridescent power. When her mother and brother tried to duck under the limbs to get to Jovi, they were pushed back as the limbs became ferocious arms.

The wind picked up, howling through the branches of the quaking willow. Jovi heard a voice in the wind. It was the one she often heard calling to her. But this time it was unmistakable —the words clear and loud as the currents of warm air carried them to her.

'Across the heavens I have blown, my power harnessed, now your own.'

Jovi reached a hand out to touch the ethereal voice. It was all around her. She lifted her hands and felt an overwhelming power fill her. The wind changed direction, swirling furiously around her like a funnel, waiting for her command. Jovi let her hands drop to her sides and the wind vanished as suddenly as it had kicked up.

Vida darted through the willowy limbs and scooped up her daughter. She crumpled to the ground with Jovi clutched in her arms while she muttered incoherently in her native tongue.

Talon joined them, hugging both his mother and sister, bathed in the shade of the gently swaying willow tree. "What in the name of the gods was that?" he asked.

"It cannot be. It cannot be!" Vida sobbed.

"Mama, I'm okay," Jovi murmured stroking her mother's tear stained cheeks. "The wind didn't hurt me. I'm safe."

"No, angel you're not safe. And you never will be again."

"Tell me what just happened, Mother," Talon urged.

"Forgive me son, but I hoped it would choose you," she sobbed.

"What?"

"The wind. It's chosen Jovi. Your sister is a Pillar now. And we must never speak of it again if we wish to protect her."

"Gods above," Talon whispered, staring in awe at Jovi.

The journey home had been somber and made with haste. But all along Jovi smiled, understanding that she had been given a gift most precious.

4

Jovi smiled at the memories of that fateful visit. She was grateful the wind had chosen her. Perhaps it had known she was the only choice . . . that she would be the only survivor to carry the burden of being the wind Pillar.

She shut her eyes tight and sent up a silent prayer, asking the wind to carry her soul back to this tree should she fall in Lux. A howling wind answered, licking at her clothes and hair, making her shiver despite the sticky afternoon heat. Smiling at the wind's agreeable response, she pulled a knife from her belt and set to work carving her own name beneath her father's and brothers'. When she was finished she cut a thin wound on the tip of her index finger. It was shallow, but it bled readily. She held her finger to her name on the willow's trunk and stained it red, commanding her soul to find its way home when the end came.

5

Although she wished for more time, Jovi collected herself and rose to her feet. As she moved to leave the secluded shelter of the weeping boughs, they parted for her. She turned back, stroking the soft limbs of the tree.

"Thank you for your strength," she whispered. "I'll make you proud."

The Looking Glass and the Lullaby

A SHORT STORY

C.J. Benjamin

FOREWORD

Glitter and glass reflecting to me,
The darkest of dreams I ever did see.
Sing to me softly of what shall not be,
A lullaby of doomed futures for thee.
Lift the veil let the fog flee,
And I will succumb to never be free.

PROLOGUE

There once were two daughters sent from above,
Gifted and cursed despite their mother's fierce love.
One born of the moon a child darker than none,
One born with lightness only rivaled by the sun.
Together their powers could set the world free,
But alas together they were not meant to be.

1

Jemma stared at her reflection in the mirror. She shuddered at the ghostly images that faded in and out behind the thin surface of glass. She closed her eyes tightly in effort to shut them out. It had always been like this. Her trying to see herself, but her reflection full of sullen ghosts calling to her, whispering the darkest grievances of her soul.

She still remembered the first time she realized that this wasn't normal—that *she* wasn't normal.

It was when her mother caught her singing a lullaby to her sister. Before her world had been stolen away . . .

Jemma rested her hands against the sink basin for support and pressed her forehead against the cool surface of the mirror letting her memories flood over her.

JEMMA KNELT NEXT to the woven bassinet and gazed down at her sister's snow-white complexion. She was fussing again. Jemma ran her fingers across the fragile skin of the baby's soft cheek.

"Shhh, it's okay, Eva. Don't cry. You'll wake Mama."

But Jemma's baby sister continued to fuss, staring up at her with clear blue eyes full of tears.

"Do you want to hear a song, Eva?"

The baby hiccupped. Jemma took that as a yes and she began to sing.

"Hush, hush little baby. Don't make a sound.
If you cry any louder they will come from the ground.
Shhh, shhh my dear one. You must be brave.
For the moon is full and they already dig our grave.
Sing, sing sweet child, call to the bones.
The war is coming, certain as the stones."

All at once Eva stopped crying and the tent was bathed in silence. The strange absence of sound was unsettling. So much so that Jemma turned to check if her mother was still sleeping because she no longer heard the steady rise and fall of her breath. Jemma looked to the bed, but her mother, Nesia, was no longer asleep. She sat on the edge of the bed—spine straight, eyes wide with terror.

"Mama?"

"Where did you learn that song, Jemma?" her mother whispered.

"From the man."

"What man?"

"The man in the looking glass," Jemma said proudly.

2

Nesia was on her feet. She darted to her vanity and pulled her looking glass from its velvet case. She held it out to Jemma. "Can you show me?"

Jemma bit her lip and shook her head. She had a sinking feeling that she was in trouble. She knew she wasn't supposed to play with her mother's looking glass. It was a gift from her father. But Jemma found the treasure irresistible. It had a delicate ivory handle carved to look like a goddess surrounded by a vine of roses that climbed the mirror's gold frame. And every time Jemma gazed into the mirror she saw someone else. All different kinds of people and places lived in the mirror and Jemma looked forward to their conversations. They told her all kinds of things. But her favorite was the lullaby an old man had shared with her.

"Please, baby? I won't be mad," Nesia pleaded as her trembling hands stroked the black curtain of Jemma's hair. "I promise."

Jemma placed her tiny hand around the handle of the looking glass her mother offered. She gazed into the reflective pool of glass, letting her mother kneel behind her. For a moment Jemma only caught her own reflection. She looked harder and the shadows began to form like dark clouds colliding.

"It's okay," Jemma whispered. "You can come out now."

Nesia's heart hammered as she silently watched her daughter speak to the looking glass. She couldn't see anything abnormal in the reflection, but obviously Jemma did.

"You don't have to be scared," Jemma murmured. "I told her about you. She promised not to be mad." Jemma turned her dark, hopeful eyes to her mother, looking at her for confirmation. "Do you want to talk to them, Mama?"

3

Nesia's face was full of tears. She'd been warned this would happen, but she didn't want to believe it. She'd kept her daughters hidden hoping to protect them, but it was evident that the prophecy was coming true and she couldn't outrun it.

She tore the looking glass from Jemma's hand and shouted into it. "Leave my children alone!" And then with all her might, Nesia smashed the mirror against the ground, shattering the glass into dangerous shards.

Jemma cried out and Nesia pulled her into her arms, holding her tightly against her chest as she sank to the ground. She rocked her sobbing daughter back and forth, cursing the danger that had lured her daughter in.

"Mama! Why did you do that? Those were my friends."

"They're not your friends, Jemma. You need to stay away from them."

"Why?"

"Because they want to hurt you."

"No they don't! They tell me stories and show me where secrets are hidden."

"No, darling. The shadows you see in the looking glass are bad and if you spend too much time with them, they'll make you bad too."

Jemma's lower lip quivered. "But I don't want to be bad, Mama."

"I know, darling. I know."

Geneva had begun crying and Nesia scooped her up and pulled Jemma close to her again. Nesia held both her sobbing daughters and began to cry. She was out of time and she needed to make a decision. She'd known from the moment her children were born that they were fated for very different outcomes in life. One would bring light and one darkness. And now that Jemma had shown she could see through the veils to the inbetween, her fate had been sealed.

Although her darling daughters were nestled warmly in her arms, Nesia already began to mourn their loss. She knew there was no other way. She had to put an end to the darkness. It would come looking for them no matter where they hid.

Nesia closed her eyes and prayed for forgiveness. For she was about to bring her daughters to Jaka and hand them over to their destiny.

4

As Jemma revisited her childhood memories, the thoughts of that day swam in her mind. She remembered when her mother brought them to Jaka—and everything changed.

It was the last time Jemma had seen her mother alive.

"I miss you, Mama," Jemma sobbed, pushing her hands against the cold glass of the mirror above the sink basin. "I just want to go home."

"Not too much longer now," a voice called back to her.

Jemma's eyes snapped open. She'd know that voice anywhere. It was her mother.

"Mama?" she cried straining to see her mother among the dark shrouded figures in the mirror. But she wasn't there. Jemma had never been able to see Nesia on her own. She needed Geneva for that. But Geneva had abandoned her, and rightfully so. Jemma had betrayed her—her own sister.

When tears blurred her vision too much to see, Jemma gave up her hopeless search in the mirror and slid to the damp stone floor of the dungeon that held her captive. She'd lost track of the time she'd been here, locked somewhere beneath the

Tower of Lux. She lived in fear of the day Kobel would return. She didn't know what he wanted with her, but it couldn't be anything good. Darkness seeped from the man like a vapor of doom.

"Mama, I'm scared," Jemma whispered to the emptiness of her room.

"I'm here with you, darling."

"I can't do this anymore, Mama."

"I'll come for you soon, darling. And I'll carry you home on gentle black wings."

"Promise?"

"I promise. Sleep, my darling. We'll be together soon."

"Will you sing me a lullaby?"

"Which one?"

"You know the one."

Nesia's ethereal voice filled the cell, echoing the haunting melody while Jemma closed her eyes.

"Hush, hush little baby. Don't make a sound.
If you cry any louder they will come from the ground.
Shhh, shhh my dear one. You must be brave.
For the moon is full and they already dig our grave.
Sing, sing sweet child, call to the bones.
The war is coming, certain as the stones."

5

Jemma fell asleep to her mother's eerie lullaby. She dreamt of faraway places. Of a different life. One where she and Geneva were true sisters, with nothing but love between them.

When a scraping of stone startled Jemma awake, she'd forgotten for a moment where she was. But the moment her eyes found his, it all came crashing back. Kobel smiled down at Jemma tragically. His rotten grey teeth made her skin crawl. He reached his hand down to help her to her feet and she recoiled.

"Come now, Miss Sommers. There's no need to fear. Today is the day you've been dreaming of."

Jemma scrambled to her feet as two Luxors crowded the cell moving toward her. They unchained her ankles from the floor shackles and bound her hands with tight uncomfortable rope.

"Where are you taking me?" Jemma asked cowering as Kobel approached her with a menacing looking hood.

"We're going to take a nice ride to the square. Your sister is waiting for you there."

"Why?"

"You're going to help me teach her a lesson," Kobel purred slipping the hood over Jemma's face.

Jemma trembled as her world went dark. Her quivering breath heated the suffocating air beneath the heavy hood. Her body involuntarily shivered as Kobel's hand met her back, guiding her from the cell. Jemma tried to be brave but something deep within her bones told her she was marching to her death.

Jemma began to sob. But then Kobel's voice slithered to her ear.

"Shhh, shhh my dear one. You must be brave."

And then the world disappeared.

ALSO BY C.J. BENJAMIN

YOUNG ADULT FANTASY/DYSTOPIAN SERIES

Geneva Sommers and the Quest for Truth (Book 1)

Geneva Sommers and the Secret Legend (Book 2)

Geneva Sommers and the Myth of Lies (Book 3)

Geneva Sommers and the Magic Destiny (Book 4)

Geneva Sommers and the First Fairytales (Prequels)

ABOUT THE AUTHOR

Award-Winning author, C.J. Benjamin, lives in Florida with her husband, and character inspiring pets, where she spends her free time working on her books and speaking to inspire fellow writers.

Her best-selling novel, *Geneva Sommers and the Quest for Truth,* has won multiple awards and stolen the hearts of YA readers everywhere. Packed with magic and imagination, her epic tale of adventure hooks fans of mega-hit YA fiction like Harry Potter, The Hunger Games and Percy Jackson.

C.J. Benjamin loves to read and write across genres. She also writes YA contemporary romance under the name, Christina Benjamin.

For more information visit
www.crownatlanticpublishing.com

www.ingramcontent.com/pod-product-compliance
Lightning Source LLC
Chambersburg PA
CBHW030531310726
48979CB00010B/1873/J

* 9 7 8 1 7 3 2 6 1 2 3 9 6 *